I Am Forbidden

I Am Forbidden

A Novel

ANOUK MARKOVITS

HOGARTH

LONDON · NEW YORK

Published by Hogarth 2012

2 4 6 8 10 9 7 5 3 1

First published in Great Britain in 2012 by
Hogarth, an imprint of Chatto & Windus
Random House, 20 Vauxhall Bridge Road,
London SW1V 2SA
www.randomhouse.co.uk

Addresses for companies within The Random House Group Limited can be found at:
www.randomhouse.co.uk/offices.htm

The Random House Group Limited Reg. No. 954009

A CIP catalogue record for this book
is available from the British Library

ISBN 9781781090022

The Random House Group Limited supports The Forest Stewardship Council (FSC®),
the leading international forest certification organisation. Our books carrying the
FSC label are printed on FSC® certified paper. FSC is the only forest certification
scheme endorsed by the leading environmental organisations, including Greenpeace.
Our paper procurement policy can be found at www.randomhouse.co.uk/environment

To Larry Berger

The Law's parchment once was skin, the thread was sinew, the quill once flew and I—

I am forbidden, so are my children and my children's children, forbidden for ten generations male or female.

Tell me, scroll of fire, how one learns to be already written. Tell me, scroll of ashes, how one begins anew.

Book I

Szatmár, Transylvania

LIGHT, FAST, ZALMAN'S HEELS RAPPED THE GROUND as he ran, naked, down the centre aisle of the House of Prayer. His hand reached towards the Torah scroll raised above the altar, but the embroidered mantle slid up and out of sight. The scroll spread open, revealing a passage he had not memorised. There, supine on the black Ashurite script, her long plaits undone, was Rachel Landau, the bride of his study partner. Her dark eyes smiled at Zalman. He ran faster towards her, his hips rose and fell, circling the heat in his ammah—

Zalman awoke to a damp warmth on his thigh. He lay still, as the texts he knew so well descended upon him: *You who inflame yourselves among the terebinths ... who slay the children in the valley ... No, do not read* shochtay, *who slay, but* sochtay, *who cause to flow. Rabbi Yochanan says, Whoever emits seed in vain deserves death.* Zalman tugged at the belt strapped around his wrists. If his roommates had not been there, he would have beaten his chest, heeding the command: *Become angry and do not sin.* He pressed the buckle against the pillow so it would not clang against the brass headboard. He disengaged one wrist, then the other. He had taken every precaution — neither Law nor custom commanded that he bind his hands. He unwound the string tying his ankle to the footboard to prevent him from turning onto his belly and rubbing accidentally during sleep. He reached for the water and washbowl. The clammy pyjamas hugged his groin.

Master of the universe, I have done this unwittingly.

He pulled off the sheet.

Every bed, whereon he lieth that hath the issue, is unclean.

He stole down the stairs, into the unlit, narrow alley where each slat of the closed shutters was an accusation. In the desert, he would have been barred from the Tabernacle's camp and from the Levites' camp.

He pushed open the low door to the ritual bath. He would immerse himself three times and then he would be permitted to study the holy books that same day — *born anew after the third immersion.*

He disrobed. The water nipped at his calves, his thighs; the chill shrivelled his ammah. He spread his arms and let himself sink, to make sure his long sidecurls were submerged.

It had happened in his sleep, Zalman reasoned; he was sure he had never run, naked, in front of a woman's eyes, but he was guilty in other ways and the Lord was punishing him — surely his classmates were not visited by such dreams.

He should have fled as soon as he saw Gershon holding a pushpin and a Talmud tome, as soon as he saw the assembled students. The metal point hovered above a line of text, careful not to scratch the holy letters, then it stilled above the word *father*.

'Nu, Zalman?' the students coaxed.

Zalman did not resist. 'Strife.'

Gershon held up the page of the heavy treatise and all the heads bowed to inspect which word was on the reverse side of the page, exactly where the pin was pointing: *strife*.

Already the pushpin hovered above another word.

'Two pages from here, Zalman?'

He should have called it vanity and turned away but he knew the word to which the pin was pointing two pages ahead. '*Behold.*' Only when the pin hovered above a third word did Zalman put an end to the conceit, but even as he hurried away, he took pleasure in his classmates' reverent whispers.

Zalman's head broke the surface of the water for one breath, then he sank a second time, drifting deeper into his past.

Ezra the Pedlar called out to him: 'Six years old and you can name Adam's offspring all the way to King David? What was the name of Adam's twelfth-generation descendant?'

'Arphachsad.'

'The twenty-fifth?'

'Amram.'

'It's true, the Stern boy is an ilui, a wonder of Torah knowledge.'

Zalman had not known how to be modest. He blurted out the twenty-sixth name and the twenty-seventh as if the Lord's gift were a personal achievement.

. .˙ .

Zalman lifted his head for a second breath, and sank under the water a third time.

His father's words boomed: 'Five years old and our son plays marbles instead of studying?'

When the teacher had left the class room, Zalman had sprung up with the other boys to pitch walnuts and measure whose was closest to the wall.

His father's worry; his mother's silence.

Zalman sank towards the bottom of the small pool until he turned three, a child with a child's set of obligations. His father sheared his hair, leaving two sidecurls. Then he began to float upward and he was two, spelling his first words while raisins and almonds rained from Heaven. He was one, licking Hebrew letters coated with honey while his mother smothered him in kisses. He rose out of the water.

Born anew.

Now he could put on his phylacteries, now he could beseech Him: *Remember the binding of Isaac and Your promise to Abraham. In their merit not mine, subdue, kill, uproot the Lilin that were spawned through these drops that left me in vain . . .*

The Lord heard Zalman's supplication. There were no nocturnal emissions during the Days of Awe leading to the Day of Atonement, nor from the Day of Atonement to the Feast of Tabernacles. Once more, Zalman looked every man straight in the eye. On the night of the Festival of the Law, Simchath Torah, Zalman danced. Never had Zalman felt His presence with such immediacy.

. . .

4

Until sundown the previous eve, the Hasidim had discussed Hitler and Stalin marching across the newspapers; they had argued about the fall of Warsaw ten days earlier, and about Poland partitioned, but on the Festival of the Law, the Hasidim danced. Their right arms rose, folded, unfolded, drumming the air that circled the scroll that circled their years. Each round heaved their bodies closer to their souls.

Leading the dance, the Rebbe tossed his head from side to side. Eyes closed, the Rebbe saw wonders words could not convey. He skipped and the heart of the whole congregation leapt.

'Shaddaï! Melech! Netzach!' the Rebbe cried out.

The circling stilled, the Hasidim shuddered as the Lord's names hovered above their lifted faces.

'Aye yaï yaï,' the Rebbe called.

'Aye yaï yaï yaï,' his Hasidim responded. They sang tune after tune, they hummed melodies unconstrained by word or meaning, and their sidecurls were silver streams twirling in front of Heaven's gates, which surely, tonight, would swivel open on the seventh round.

His assistant whispered into the Rebbe's ear, the Rebbe nodded, the assistant called, '"Adir Kevodo" will be sung by Zalman Stern!'

It was a great honour to lead an anthem in the Rebbe's court, an immense distinction for an unmarried youth, but Zalman was not only a wonder of Torah knowledge, he also had the most beautiful voice east of Vienna.

'Shaah! Quiet!' the assistant hollered.

Zalman's voice rose, focused, from his belly, as taught by his father, the cantor of Temesvár. *'Splendid is His honour...'*

The notes plunged deep and then kept climbing,

spurring the men's longing to break free from their bodies. They joined for the refrain, startled to hear their unruly modulations cover the perfect pitch.

Then Zalman's voice soared again.

Long after the last note had lingered and died, all were still, until the Rebbe let out an *'Aye mamale aye!'*

They leaned into the dance – the boys, the men in their prime, the men with white beards; hugging the Torah scrolls, they skipped along the ring that wheeled their past into their future; entwined by their sidecurls, they wound themselves back to *In the Beginning*.

Dawn was breaking when the men left the synagogue.

Zalman Stern and his study partner, Gershon Heller, left together. The two youths walked in a fashion that showed respect for the Lord's presence: not too proud, shoulders back and chin out, but not bent over. Their steps tapped lightly through the fog. They parted before reaching Piaţa Libertăţii. Zalman entered the large square alone. Strips of haze swathed the façades, but Zalman saw sparkling gems: If, on Simchath Torah, dancing was akin to prayer; if, on Simchath Torah, angels gathered every step danced by every Jew and wove them into crowns, then the Lord's splendour, this morning—

Something pulled at Zalman's collar, hard, from behind.

A muffled pop. A receding clink as a button ricocheted against the cobblestones.

Soldiers.

A tug on Zalman's sleeve. Two more buttons snapped.

A muzzle lifted his hat. His hand came to his head.

Blunt thump on his fingers. Zalman's hand retreated,

but not before tapping the skullcap to make sure it had remained in place.

The muzzle pointed to the ground. 'Pick it up!'

Zalman picked up his hat, held it with both hands, not sure whether to place it back on his head.

A pair of black leather boots advanced. Two leather fingers pinched the hat, lifted it, slowly. A palm flattened the hat onto Zalman's skull. The boots stepped back.

A bayonet pointed to his belly.

Zalman closed his eyes. If he was to die, then let him meet death in the manner of Rabbi Akivah, uttering the word *One*. Like the martyrs before him, Zalman intoned: '*Hear, O Israel: the Lord is our God, the Lord is*—'

'One, two, three. Stand still!' a voice in front commanded.

A click. A flash.

Zalman's shoulders were hunched. He was looking to the pavement, coat gaping, hat crushed on his forehead as the soldiers around him held a triumphant pose.

The same voice in front: 'Nice. One more. Don't move!'

Click, flash.

The soldiers relaxed their rifles, the photographer folded his tripod, the squad stepped into the fog that still blanketed the façades of Piaţa Libertăţii.

Zalman's eyes opened wide. His heart soared.

He had been ready, ready to die in the Lord's name.

★

A FEW MONTHS later, Zalman Stern married Hannah Leah Shaïovits and the guilty dreams never returned. Emitting his seed as commanded, Zalman begat his first child whom he named Eydell Atara — Eydell in memory of his mother's mother, Atara for the crowns he saw the morning his life was spared.

The story of the photograph was the only one Zalman would tell his children, to stand in for the next five un-photographable years.

Maramureş, Transylvania

A HUNDRED KILOMETRES EAST OF SZATMÁR, ON THE morning Zalman's life was spared, five-year-old Josef Lichtenstein sat on the kitchen stool and watched his mother tie a ribbon in his little sister's hair. He tried to follow Mama's fingers as they folded the ribbon under, over, as they pinched a curl, but he could not puzzle out how the strip of fabric bloomed into a four-loop bow atop Pearela's head.

A branch brushed the pane, the frames of the half-open window tapped lightly, a leaf – flame shaped and autumn red – twirled into the kitchen. Josef scrambled down the stool and twirled after the leaf.

In her high chair, Pearela leaned to the side, reaching for Josef.

'Jossela, why don't you play with your little sister in the hall while I get breakfast ready.'

Mama lifted Pearela out of the high chair. Josef took hold of his baby sister's hand.

'Leave the door open so I can see you.'

Sitting cross-legged on the hall's parquet, Josef raised the hinged lid of a cardboard box and held up a Hebrew letter carved out of wood. 'Look Pearela, *la-med, l-l-lamed.*'

Pearela reached for the letter. 'La! La!' She fell back, bounced up, and chirping like a sparrow, toddled down the corridor.

Josef rushed to close the door to the dining room with the overhanging tablecloth, which Pearela had already pulled down, twice. 'Mama said you mustn't!'

The catch of the lock did not hold. Pearela pushed open the door, reached towards the table, toppled onto the carpet.

'Jossela! Pearela! Milk, walnut roll!' Mama called from the kitchen.

Leaning to help his sister up, Josef saw a wooden letter he had thought lost. He crawled under the table and clasped the letter's branch. 'Beth! Look Pearela' – he laid out the two letters on the carpet – '*lamed, beth.*'

'La!' Pearela chirped.

'Tatta says lamed is the *last* letter of the Torah, beth is the *first* letter, together they make the word – bring back the letter, Pearela!'

Springing up in pursuit of his little sister, Josef whacked his forehead against the edge of the table. He fell back under the table, held his breath, reminded himself that a five-year-old boy was old enough not to cry.

'Jossela! Pearela!' their mother called again.

Heavy steps. Not Mama. Not Tatta. Not Florina.

A smell of hog and swamp. Mud on the carpet.

Frayed shoes splayed inches from his nose.

One prong pierced Pearela's cheek, the other split her chest. The green-and-pink checks of Pearela's dress turned red. Screams rose in the yard. The shoes stepped to the window, spattering. A gritty throat clearing, a ball of spit hit the sill. The shoes left the room, precipitously.

The screams in the yard intensified. They stopped.

The heavy steps, hairy shins.

Mama's shoes dangling from the string belt that held the tattered trousers.

The hayfork leaned against the table, prongs glistening red. A drawer creaked. All the drawers creaked. Dirt-rimmed nails clamped the foot of a chair, which soared out of sight. The sideboard glided away. The hayfork leaned against the wall. The table lifted above Josef's head, an inch.

A grunt, the table dropped; lifted and dropped, three times. A swear word. Josef recognised the man's voice: Octavian the smith with the armband, who often bragged about joining the Romanian Iron Guard.

The hayfork lurched away.

Josef waited for his sister's soft warble. He clutched the remaining wooden letter and did not move. Pearela's dress grew darker.

It was night, then it was day. A gold curl escaped the crusted, maroon sheath that now encased Pearela.

The chant of harvesters leaving for the fields.

A soft tap-tap, dusty black shoes, men from the Jewish Burial Society, stepping onto the carpet, removing Pearela, gently.

The chant of harvesters returning from the fields.

Florina scrubbing the carpet on her knees, which meant that Mama would be there to pay her weekly wages.

The brush was inches from Josef's feet when Florina lifted her eyes. She saw him under the table, alive. Her jaw dropped. She crossed herself.

The fat bolt slid in its socket, the windows banged shut. Florina reached for him and took him in her arms.

She removed his velvet skullcap. She cut his sidecurls.

She wrapped him in his mother's eiderdown and carried him to the horse cart. She lifted a cloth bundle from the driver's bench, dropped it onto the cart bed, set him on the bench, hauled herself next to him.

Wind gusting through dry leaves spurred the horse's trot and Florina's Ave Marias, all night long.

FLORINA HAD KNOWN the boy since before he was born. She had watched over him in his parents' backyard; lying on a soft blanket, she had dug her nose behind his ears to smell his clean skin and good clothes. She had gazed into his eyes, green and prickly topside, grey and downy underside — wood-nettle eyes, she called them.

When the boy was three, his father had shaved his golden hair, leaving the two devilish sidecurls. Still, she had day-dreamed she would baptise the boy, where the river looped round the willows.

The sun was high in the sky when Florina turned to Josef. 'Your name is Anghel. Your father left for the Odessa front before you were born. You are my son.'

The boy looked at the maid, her flowery scarf, her gleaming medallion of the archangel Michael slaying the dragon-Jew, which she had shown him in secret but now wore over her blouse. His hand came up to the fresh stubble where his sidecurls used to be. Never again would Mama spool them onto rollers, proudly, while he recited his bedtime prayers.

NIGHT HAD FALLEN for the third time when they stopped in front of a wooden gate.

'My mother's farm,' Florina said.

A peasant raised a lantern above the cart bed crammed with furniture. He chuckled.

'They robbed us long enough,' Florina said.

The man leaned his stubbly jaw to Florina's face. 'Did you see, on your way in?'

Florina crossed herself. 'The earth was swelling . . . scabbing . . . we heard groans and—'

'Prostie! They should make sure they're dead, they should let the bodies cool.' Again, the farmhand raised his lantern above the cart bed. 'You weren't afraid?'

'Petrified. The trees were chasing us—'

'I mean, to work for them. Don't you know Jews sell Christian women?'

Florina laughed. 'Not the ones I worked for.'

His vexed grumble. 'I didn't think you'd be back.'

A silence.

'Help me with my boy,' Florina said. 'He's asleep.'

'Your *what*?'

'Hush!'

'You married!'

'I had to.'

'His father—'

'Is dead,' Josef said.

Carrying the boy into the kitchen, Florina looked over her shoulder, then she whispered in his ear, 'Never take off your trousers in front of anyone. Ever.'

The boy stared at his mother's brooch, fastened on Florina's pinafore.

'Mama is dead,' he said.

'Hush!'

Florina took off a skirt. Florina never undressed entirely, she did not have a white nightgown, a pale blue

13

quilted bed-jacket. She did not read in bed, did not know how to read. She took off her kerchief, black since she called him Anghel, my son, husband killed, Odessa front. The bed tilted when she sat on it. He rolled towards her on the soft incline, came to a stop against her wide backside. His feet nested between her calves.

In the kitchen's four-poster bed, Florina and the boy curled up for the night. Under the eiderdown in which he still smelled his mother's sleep, Florina lulled him: *'To live, Mama wants Anghel to live ...'*

Florina and the boy cut through the cat's-tails as bells called across the fields. She looked over her shoulder, stopped.

'You'll sit when I sit, you'll stand when I stand, and when the priest places the wafer on your tongue, you'll ask Christ to forgive you. Soon we'll go to the river and you won't have to be a Jew anymore.' She smiled. 'After you are baptised, you too will fly to Heaven.'

'In Heaven, I will see Mama—'

'Hush!'

They walked, silent, through the tall grass.

Every Sunday, the bearded priest paced in front of the pews swinging a censer that released, with each oscillation, a tangy cloud of myrrh. Behind the cloud, the cassock's black sleeves puffed up like wings straining to unfold, the walls swelled with light, the icons' eyes were furry bees, *In this joyous Eucharistic liturgy, in resurrectional felicity, in this bread, in this wine ... burn me with longing, O Christ!*

Anghel took Jesus's body on his tongue, and His Blood, and God cried tears of gold and Anghel learned that Jews were responsible for what befell them, because Jews refused to see the light.

Winter. Spring.

After Florina left to milk the cows, Anghel set out with the eiderdown. He picked daisies, anemones, bluebells, buttercups. As he had seen Florina do, he placed the bouquet at the base of the field shrine behind the vegetable patch.

'Pearela,' he whispered, staring at the red-brown rivulets on Jesus's bony toes. The gnarled knees and scrawny thighs were entirely different from his baby sister's cuddly limbs, but those nailed palms surely knew of Pearela with the prong in her cheek. He swaddled the thin ankles and rusty nails with one end of the eiderdown and wrapped himself in the other end.

'Hie lee lu lee la,' he hummed softly.

The first warm rays grazed the ridge when Florina lifted eiderdown and sleeping boy. She carried them into the kitchen. She smiled as her broad hand rubbed hot tuica on Anghel's chest, but the boy was careful not to smile back, fully smile. If his dimple showed, Florina might think he was trying to bewitch her, she might tap his forehead to gauge whether he had grown his Jew horns, she might wonder whether he was, in fact, stealing what she was giving him.

Summer, a fence was erected behind the shrine, along the tracks skirting the horse meadow. On this side of the fence was Romania; on the other side was Hungary. On this side of the fence, men started to wear the armband of the Legion of the Archangel Michael, the Iron Guard.

Winter, Anghel learned to hitch the oxen to the plough. He learned that he liked to lead them to the field, to feel their warm hides, that they talked in hollow moans. But he never shared his midday meal with the field hands. Instead, he went to his hideout in the bluff where he sat and watched the leaves falling together, and landing apart.

★

THEN IT WAS spring again and maybe they were butter-flies, the white flickerings along the sealed boxcars, maybe they were not fingers begging for water, and his name was Anghel whose father died in Odessa, whose mother was Florina who pressed her medallion every morning to his forehead and coached: 'You will not be first in class. If you understand, don't show it. Don't answer the teacher's questions.'

★

THE DOGS BARKED before the cockerel crowed. Anghel rose from bed and looked out the kitchen window. He saw three silhouettes emerge from the mist above the river. He hushed the dogs.

After Florina left with the wheelbarrow and the rake, he set out for the shed in the meadow – where else would the fugitives have gone without alerting the neighbour's hounds? He started and stopped on the sodden earth to forestall its sucking sounds. He crouched against the shed's wall and placed an eye to a chink between two logs.

A man, a woman, a little girl.

The man was fastening a black cube to his forehead. His lips moved as he swayed back and forth. The woman was sitting on the floor, her back against the wall. She was tying a blue ribbon in the girl's hair. The woman raised her head at the sound of an approaching train. The train slowed around the bend, hissed, gathered speed. The woman's hands came to her face. The man whispered in a language Anghel had not known he still remembered. The woman sighed. The little girl fell asleep in the woman's lap.

Another train approached, slowed around the bend, stopped.

The man and the woman exchanged a frightened glance. The man's torso swayed more quickly, back and forth. His lips moved again.

One hand pressing her lower back, the other flat

against the wall, the woman hauled herself up. She was pregnant, very pregnant. She peeked out of the shed's window. 'It's him, the Rebbe, quick!' The woman's face beamed.

The man's brow lifted in bewilderment. He held on to the little girl as the door of the shed scraped open.

The woman ran to the train, a train of boxcars with wide-open doors and people milling about inside.

'Rebbe!' the woman called to a Jew who sat in one of the openings, reading a book.

One shot. The woman's hand came to her chest, to the spreading stain. She stumbled.

The man rushed out of the shed, the black cube on his forehead.

Horses neighing, hooves bucking, Hungarian guards toppling the fence, crossing the Nadăş River.

The little girl stood in the shed's doorway.

Anghel's hand came down on her mouth. Her muffled cry under his palm, 'Mama!', as he pulled her behind the shed, to the ground, as he told her not to move, that her mother wanted her to live.

The train pulled away.

After nightfall, Anghel and the little girl crossed the trampled fence.

Peasants from nearby villages were dismantling market stalls and loading the parts onto carts. One peasant told, over and over, how the militiamen had whipped the fleeing Jew, how the Jew had let out an astonishing cry. A bottle passed from hand to hand. There were belches and cheers, for the land that soon would be cleansed of Jews.

In the market square, the girl's father was tied to a post.

His shoulders folded forward, his head drooped. Sweat drew his beard and sidecurls to a point. The arms, thighs, shins were slashed — it was impossible to see; it was impossible not to see, where the legs met, the split flesh where blood spurted through crusted blood.

Three men in the Arrow Cross uniform kept guard, their black boots stomping the mess of crimson sawdust.

In the recess where they hid, Anghel and the little girl heard the moan: 'Wasser . . .'

The girl dashed to the village pipe, cupped her hands.

Anghel pulled her back, held her face against his chest.

'Tatta . . .' the girl stammered as water dripped through her fingers.

After the last militiaman had disappeared inside the tavern, the two children crossed the square. The girl brought her cupped hands to her father's lips. 'Tatta . . .'

The folded figure moaned, licked water from her fingers. Blood came out of the man's mouth, and words: '*Mi-la*, your name now is *Mila*. Go to Zalman Stern . . .'

Another gush of blood and words: 'With my own, see to it, see that Gershon Heller is buried with his own.'

'I will,' the boy whispered and his hand pressed the girl's mouth to his chest, to his shirt of coarse linen, so her whimper would not be heard.

The tavern door opened. Anghel pulled the girl past the bullwhip and the wound. He led her to his hollow in the bluff where they heard Florina call across the fields.

'Anghel! Anghel!' And again, 'Anghel! Anghel!'

. . .

When all the lights in the village had gone dark, the two children returned to the market square. The body had been untied from the post; it lay across the tray of a wheelbarrow. The boy took hold of the shafts and pulled. Behind, leaning against the barrow's rim, the little girl pushed.

Under the poplars at the bottom of the sloping meadow, the boy loosened the earth with his shovel. The little girl scooped the soil with her bare hands. Together they pulled and pushed the body into the shallow grave. The boy heaped earth over the body; the little girl helped. When they were done, the boy said, 'Later, I'll see that he is buried in the Jewish cemetery.'

The girl nodded. Then: 'Tatta said if anything happens I must go to Zalman Stern in Nagyszeben. The train will say Sibiu but it's the same as Nagyszeben. If I can't get on the train I must run from the border. Tatta said I must run right away.'

'I'll help you get on. Don't be afraid, all the trains go slow around the bend. I'll jump on over there. You'll wait here. When I come by, grab my hand. Don't be afraid. I'll pull you up fast. Just look at my hand. If the conductor comes by, say you lost your ticket. No, say your parents are in the next carriage. Say it in Hungarian and don't speak the Jew language. You'll know when to get off when the conductor calls, "Sibiu!"'

The boy brushed the dirt off her coat. He tied the ribbon in her hair.

'Mila,' she said, pointing to her chest.

'Anghel,' he said, pointing to his chest.

'Where is your mother?' Mila asked.

'Florina—'

'Your mother, where is she?'

'Mama is dead. Tatta is dead. Pearela is dead.'

'*Shayfeleh* . . .' Mila's hand stroked Anghel's cheek, and he remembered that it meant little lamb.

Sibiu, Southern Transylvania

THE STERN CHILDREN WERE NOT TO OPEN THE front door, so when four-year-old Atara heard the knock, she ran to her mother in the kitchen.

A little girl was standing in the doorway, her coat torn, a dirty ribbon in her hair.

Hannah squinted at the child. 'Mila Heller? The daughter of Gershon and Rachel?' Hannah took the little girl in her arms. 'Zalman! Come quickly!'

The little girl collapsed.

Hannah would tell so many times the story of Mila's knock — blessed be the Lord who kept watch over the little girl, how else did a child so young find the right train, how did she find her way from the railway station to their home? Hannah would tell so many times how she washed the soil out of Mila's hair, how she scoured the heavy dirt from under Mila's nails, that Hannah's children born years later thought they remembered five-year-old Mila Heller arriving on their doorstep.

Hannah also told of Mila's silence. 'What happened to your parents, child?'

All summer long, Mila Heller did not speak. But she

did cry at night in the bed she shared with Atara, and Atara held her hand.

On the eve of the Day of Atonement, Hannah circled a cockerel above the boys' heads, three times, then she circled a hen over the girls' heads, three times. She lowered the cackling fowl to the ground. 'Place your foot on its neck,' Hannah coached Mila.

Mila shook her head, no.

'Surely you remember this from home,' Hannah said. 'You need not press on it. Just brush your foot against its head and repeat after me: *You to death and I to life* . . . do it.' Then, softly: 'You don't have to say it aloud, child, but think it to yourself.'

Tears filled Mila's eyes.

Atara cried out: 'Why does the chicken have to die?'

'So the children will not die.' Once more, Hannah lowered the fowl to the ground.

Staring into the hen's darting eye, Mila extended a shaking leg.

Hannah coached: 'You to death . . .'

Mila pulled back her leg.

'Why, why does the chicken have to die?' Atara insisted.

'So we won't die for our sins. The chicken is our Kappures. It will die instead of us.'

Atara frowned. 'But don't we empty our sins into the river?'

Hannah sighed, placed the fowl back in its crate. With her apron, she dried Mila's tears and her own.

That evening, as Atara held her breath in the dark, still surprised by the proximity of the orphan girl with

24

whom she was sharing her bed, Mila spoke: 'Atara is a pretty name.'

Mila had spoken; she had spoken to Atara.

From then on, Mila spoke to Atara every night. During the day, she was silent, but the two girls talked in the dark. Atara learned about Mila's unborn sibling, about Mila's mother running towards the open boxcar, calling, *'Rebbe!'*

Later she learned that Mila had decided she was allowed to love Hannah.

One night, Atara was half asleep when Mila asked, 'Do *you* believe me about my mama running out to save the Rebbe?'

Atara was silent. When Mila was not around, Zalman had said that Mila's mother could not have seen the Rebbe. Boxcars did not have open doors, not when they were full of Jews, not in the spring of '44, not in Hungary, Zalman had said.

'*You* Atara, do you believe me?' Mila insisted.

'I . . . maybe we should pray, now, for the coming of the messiah?' Atara liked to pray with Mila. She could tell that in Mila's prayer, the messiah's coming was not the glory of the Temple rebuilt but a kitchen with Mila's mother in it, a bedtime with the story Mila's father had not finished telling her.

Four months after Mila's arrival at the Sternses', Soviet and Romanian forces recaptured her hometown. As soon as Jews could travel again, Zalman set out to mark the sites of Jewish remains. He wanted the bones undisturbed, especially the small luz bone connecting neck to spine, the first to feel the Dew of Resurrection when Trumpets called the End of Days.

In the astonishing emptiness he found when he crossed into northern Transylvania, Zalman prayed: *Dear Lord, show me why You spared me, show me towards what end You spared Hannah and our children and the little girl, Blimela – daughter of Gershon and Rachel Heller.*

Zalman had intended to stay at the Rebbe's court, in Szatmár, after his wedding, but his parents had insisted he return home to Sibiu, south of the new border, when Transylvania was divided between Hungary and Romania, in August 1940. Unlike his yeshiva mates in Szatmár, Zalman and his community in Sibiu had not been deported.

★

ANGHEL WATCHED the Jew who stood on the ice ledge.

The Jew cast a net in the river and disagreed with himself:

'Sanhedrin 97b. Also, 98a . . . Will the dead rise naked or clothed?

'What of Isaiah 26:19? What of Ezekiel 37:12–14?'

The Jew extended his arms; he bent, extended, and drew the line draped with dangling algae. He dragged the net with the bodies, the two sisters who returned from deportation and were drowned by neighbours. He laid one body on the horse cart, then the second body. The net's leaded lip meandered through the splintered reeds. He seized the edge of the flatbed. The horse's iron shoe struck the frosted earth.

Hidden in the undergrowth, Anghel followed the Jew who followed the dray horse along the Nadăş River. The Jew continued to argue with himself:

'But Zalman, what of those who never went to the grave, whose bones are licked by wolves?

'They will not live again.

'What about Kethuboth 35b?

'Ah, on this our rabbis are *not* unanimous.'

Anghel shouldered through the bushes, onto the towpath. He stood in front of Zalman and pointed to the line of poplars. 'There. Another dead Jew.'

Zalman's gaze followed the boy's finger pointing to hardened clumps of soil.

'Yes, there,' the boy insisted.

'How do I trust this here is a Jew?' Zalman asked.

The boy pointed to Zalman's coat.

'Anyone can put on a black coat,' Zalman said.

The boy frowned.

'You mean, who but a Jew *wants* to put on such a coat?'

The boy tapped his forehead. 'He had a black cube.'

'Tefilin!'

'*"With my own,"* he said. *"See to it, see that Gershon Heller is buried with his own."*'

Zalman looked stunned. 'Gershon Heller? Heller from Cluj?'

The boy shrugged his shoulders. He pointed beyond the river. 'They came from over there but the woman ran to the train.'

'*To* the train?'

'She recognised someone.'

'When?'

'Last spring.'

'In a boxcar? . . .'

'The doors were open.'

'How is that possible?'

Again, the boy lifted his shoulders.

Zalman looked at the patch of upturned earth. 'If this here is a Jew . . .' He looked at the farm boy. 'This Jew truly said, *"See that Gershon Heller is buried with his own"*? He *said* it? Unless he requested it specifically, it is a terrible sin to exhume a body.'

'With my own. See to it, see that Gershon Heller is buried with his own.'

Zalman took the shovel from the cart and started to dig. Again, he argued with himself. Of course Gershon Heller requested it, Gershon Heller would want to be buried within close range of the Trumpets' call. 'When the dead rise, the dead in Jewish ground ... It is noble, what you are doing—' Zalman lifted his head. 'What is your name?'

The boy had disappeared.

Once more, the horse's shoes struck the earth; the wheels once more climbed the lane to the Jewish cemetery.

By the open grave, Zalman tore his coat on the right side, it was already torn closer to his heart. *El maleh rachamim, God full of compassion,* he chanted.

In the birch grove overlooking the cemetery, Anghel watched the Jew's bent silhouette through the drifting snowflakes, then he scrambled across to his hollow whose very tightness made him feel more secure. There, where memories were not forbidden, the boy curled up and listened to the Jew's shovel and to his chant.

Beyond the falling snow, a cloud, a white damask cloud, lifting ... his mother's hand reaching for him. 'Mein eigen kleiner Yiddeleh!' (*My own little Jew!*) Coy, the boy wriggles free, but the cloud is drawn aside and his mother takes hold of him and crushes him to her heart. 'Mein sheiner Yiddeleh!' (*My beautiful little Jew!*)

The cloud draws shut. Another memory, beyond the drifting snow, another damask cloud ... his baby sister's dimpled knee, her lace sock with ruffled edges, her tiny black patent shoe ... the heavy steps ... not Mama not Tatta not Florina. The rusty prongs glistening red—

A twig snapped in the wood. A lurching farmhand, breath reeking of cheap tuica? A Jew's body could not hold its blood. The boy huddled tighter, leaned forward, his nose almost touching the decaying leafage under the snow.

'Anghel! Anghel!' Florina called across the bluff, her voice muffled by the falling flakes.

Anghel rose, climbed the knoll towards the farmhouse where Florina had already lit the kitchen lamp.

★

ZALMAN RETURNED home and told Mila that he had buried her father properly, so that his journey would be less difficult at the End of Days. Mila received the news in silence, and then she uttered the first words she had ever spoken aloud to Zalman.

'The farm boy is a Jew. His father is dead. His mother is dead. Pearela is dead.'

'The Lord have mercy! What are you saying? What is the boy's name?'

'Anghel.'

'What sort of name is Anghel?'

Ordained rabbi at eighteen, Zalman could resolve intricate points of religious law. He could pronounce on agonising cases – women whose husbands were not returning from the camps yet no one bore witness to the husbands' deaths: Could the women remarry?

Men, too, came grieving. 'Reb Zalman, my wife was taken prisoner . . . she was forced, alas she was . . .'

'Are you a *cohen*? A Jew of priestly descent is forbidden to stay with his wife even if she struggled.'

'No, no! I'm not a cohen!'

'And she struggled?'

'Her cries, Reb Zalman . . .'

'Your wife struggled and there were witnesses; there is no doubt at all: Your wife is permitted to you.'

Zalman could determine who was forbidden, who permitted; who could remarry, who must wait longer; but when it came to Mila's claim that the farm boy was a Jew, Zalman sought the Rebbe's guidance.

★

Now and then, the Jew came. He stood by the grave of the little girl's father, stood and chanted. Anghel turned his head towards the chant. The reins loosened, the oxen stopped.

The Jew looked to the wide field, to the motionless plough.

The boy plucked the reins.

The oxen started, the sod rolled over without breaking, drafting another furrow. Vapour rose from the beasts' hide, denser than the fog that soon enfolded the oxen, the plough, and the boy.

★

ZALMAN EXAMINED the stamp, the block capital letters: U.S. POSTAGE. His thumb brushed the plane's vigorous wings. He inserted the paper knife in the crease of the envelope, took out the thin, airmail paper.

By His everlasting compassion, the Rebbe will soon be safe in America.

'America?'

Zalman remembered the Rebbe's harsh warnings: 'Do *not* leave Romania, Hungary, Poland. Do not abandon lands where our traditions have survived, where our yeshivas have flourished; do not abandon Torah lands for the treifenah medinah, for the Americaner den of novelty and assimilation.'

The Rebbe knows best, Zalman reminded himself. He read on.

Gershon Heller, may he rest in peace, died a martyr in the market square of ... the remains you buried must be his. The Lord will reward you with eternal life ...

As for the boy, the Rebbe insists: hidden children from God-fearing homes must be returned to our people. Do your utmost to trace his lineage ... if the boy is a Jew, retrieve him and return him to his people.

★

THE LONG harvest days came when the oat whispers before the blade. As during his previous trips, the Jew went to pray beside the graves. Anghel watched him from afar, but this time the Jew did not leave when he finished his prayer; he crossed swiftly into the field. 'Hallo! Hallo!' he called, gripping his wide-brimmed black hat.

The call rippled through the oats.

The field hands halted their sweeping strokes.

'Hallo! Hallo!'

Florina in her clogs hurried down the embankment. She placed a hand on Anghel's shoulder, pulled him back into the tall grass. The stalks closed on woman and boy.

The dogs growled when Zalman's horse cart stopped by the gate. They leapt the fence when Zalman climbed down. He scrambled back on the cart. A woman crossed the yard but did not quiet the dogs. Zalman lifted the reins, the horse trotted across the tracks and across the dismantled border.

On the driver's bench, Zalman queried in the age-old singsong of Talmudic disquisition: 'Whether it is permitted to entrust a child to unbelievers when no one knows if he will be reclaimed. If the child is not hidden, surely he will die, ruled Rabbi Oshri. Moreover, the parents may live and reclaim him, or the unbelievers may return him to a Jewish institution—

'And if the child ends up living like a Gentile, God forbid?'

34

Zalman tugged at the reins and turned the cart around. Once more, he stopped by the farm gate.

Erect on their hind legs, the dogs widened their circles, retreating to better pounce. Zalman recoiled on the driver's bench, his umbrella parried and thrust, but he held his ground and the cart did not budge.

'Cezar! Dracul!' a thin voice called at last.

The growling dogs backed into the yard.

From behind a bale of hay, Anghel watched.

The Jew stood in the shadow of the linden tree. 'Doamna Florina?' the Jew called. 'Doamna Florina!'

The Jew peeked into the hay barn; he peeked into the cowshed where the tip of Florina's black scarf flitted between her shoulders. 'Doamna Florina? I have come . . .' The Jew's hands splayed and closed as if in dialogue with each other; they pressed against his chest. 'May I ask where you married?'

Florina pulled a stained armband from a fold in her black skirt. She thrust the emblem of the Iron Guard under the Jew's nose. 'My husband, what's left of him.'

The Jew drew back. 'Ah . . . your husband is deceased? I'm sorry, Doamna Florina, what I am seeking must be elsewhere. Good day, Doamna Florina.'

The Jew climbed back into the cart.

Talmudic singsong kept Zalman company as he headed towards the town hall. 'This is the question: Must a Jew in hiding repent for smothering a crying infant if it was done to protect other lives? Rabbi Shimon Efrata said, If a person chooses to die rather than take life, that person shall be called holy. However, the one who smothers a crying infant to avoid detection and

35

save Jewish lives must not have a bad conscience, may the Almighty . . .'

★

ANGHEL CUT ACROSS the horse meadow and climbed the bluff overlooking the river. His feet dangled from his hollow as he reached for a wild anemone. Stem between his lips, he leaned back. His gaze drifted with a cloud and he thought of Florina, who called the colour of his eyes *wood-nettle,* green and prickly topside, grey and downy underside—

A black disk blotted out the sky; the disk leaned closer, spoke.

'Are you a Jew, yingeleh?'

Anghel pulled his knees to his chest, sprang up, clambered across the bluff, disappeared behind a ridge.

'Aha,' Zalman let out, 'a Romanian lad suspected of being Jewish would spit, curse, charge with his pitchfork.'

'He is here!' Anghel panted.

Florina's back stiffened. Her eyes crinkled to a slit.

The boy's lower lip trembled. 'I didn't say anything.'

A tear gathered in the boy's lashes and he confessed that two winters back, he did approach the Jew.

The dogs barked. Flick of Florina's hand, the boy disappeared.

Florina led the oxen to their stalls. She poured a bucket of water on the barn floor. The bristles scoured as Zalman paced the yard, careful to keep his distance from the dogs pulling at their chains. Florina poured a second bucket. A third. Zalman's head and beard filled the small opening in the thick mud wall. 'Is the floor not clean yet, Doamna Florina?' When the brush lifted again, Zalman said, 'Doamna Florina, for whom did you say you worked, in Vișeu de Sus?'

Zalman had established that Florina had worked for the Lichtensteins, that Iron Guard legionnaires murdered the Lichtensteins in 1939, that the Jewish Burial Society inhumed the parents and a baby girl, but the body of a five-year-old boy was never recovered.

'The boy,' Zalman whispered, 'what happened to Josef, the Lichtenstein boy?'

At last Florina came out of the barn, bucket dangling from her stiff arm. Zalman followed her to the farmhouse. The door closed on her.

Zalman knocked and stepped into the kitchen. 'Tell him, Doamna Florina, tell him what awaits him once your neighbours find out their suspicions are grounded.'

When Florina did not answer, Zalman turned to the boy. 'They will kill you if you are a Jew and usurp a farmer's inheritance.'

Zalman's eyes adjusted to the half-light. He saw the crucifix above the four-poster bed, he stepped back into the yard, where he paced determinedly, back and forth.

Florina looked to where she and the boy prayed every night.

In the kitchen with the four-poster bed, Anghel saw Florina's love and her helplessness, and it washed over him, too. They shared this moment of losing all, of having already lost.

Anghel strode out. 'What about Florina?' he asked.

Zalman stopped pacing. 'Doamna Florina is a right-eous Gentile. God will reward her a thousandfold.'

'Florina is my mother.'

'*The Lord have mercy*, you have forgotten your own mother, Josef, son of Yekutiel and Judith?'

'What will you do with me?'

'Do with you? You'll live as you were meant to live. You'll study in the Rebbe's new yeshiva in America.'

'And Florina?'

'Doamna Florina will have her share in the next world. In this world, she will not lack a thing.'

'She will not come to America?'

'Doamna Florina will not be happy where you are going.'

The boy hesitated. 'If I go with you, will I see Mama, Tatta, Pearela?'

'Child ... surely you know that your mother and father ...'

The boy tried again. 'If I go with you, I will not fly to Heaven, but if I don't fly to Heaven, will I see Mama, Tatta, Pearela?'

Zalman strode past the boy. He banged on the kitchen door. 'What have you told this child?'

Florina, in the semi-dark, did not look up. 'To live, I told my Anghel to live.'

'Doamna Florina, for a Jew, there is no other life than to live as a Jew.'

But there had been another life for Florina and Anghel. Seven years, Florina and the boy had dwelled in the kingdom where widows are faithful to their departed spouses – dead to this world but alive in Christ. Florina had been constant to the memory of her fictitious husband, she had rejected Calin's advances and Petru's, she had worn the widow's scarf, for her son, Anghel, seven years.

ONE LAST NIGHT, Florina watched over the boy's sleep, then she opened the door onto the dark and went to milk the cows.

The boy lay furled in foetal position under the eiderdown, his nose burrowing the soft peaks and crevices, hunting for his mothers' scents.

Zalman was waiting in the yard when Florina returned. He did not enter the kitchen with the crucifix but pointed from the threshold to the open suitcase. 'He won't need these where he's going.'

Florina removed the boy's new wooden clogs. She snapped shut the cardboard suitcase and tied a string around it. She flattened the eiderdown, rolled it in a tight bolt, tied a string around it. She placed his first mother's brooch in the boy's hand.

The boy clasped the brooch and wrapped his arms around the eiderdown, disappearing behind it.

Then Florina let go of the boy with the wood-nettle eyes, green topside, grey and downy underside – in the right light. She watched her Anghel and the Jew walk to the gate. Standing under the short, tin awning, she waited for her son to look back over his shoulder one last time.

They had reached the gate when Zalman told the boy that it would be better for Doamna Florina if he kept his eyes straight ahead.

Zalman spread his coat on the cart bed.

The boy huddled between Zalman's coat and the eiderdown, between black wool and white cotton as the wheels crushed the gravel, turning, turning from Florina . . .

The cart was clattering past the Jewish cemetery when Zalman said, 'Already, without any learning, you have done a good deed – the remains of Gershon Heller are in Jewish ground, ready for the End of Days. For this alone, the Lord will reward you with eternal life.' Zalman glanced back at the hump of boy and eiderdown. He looked to the road ahead. 'Vatome-er Zio-on,' Zalman chanted. 'That's how your haphtorah begins. Will you be ready for your bar mitzvah, Josef, son of Yekutiel and Judith? Bar mitzvah means son of the commandment; it means that soon, when you turn thirteen, you'll be an adult in the eyes of the Law.' As if Josef had responded, Zalman intoned the cantillations boys learn when they prepare to read aloud the Torah in synagogue: 'Zakef kato-on . . . Let your voice rise, deep, from your belly! Zakef Gadol . . . You think I'm making these up? You think man can create such blissful modulations? No, God Himself taught them to Moses on Sinai.' And to the vast silent fields, to the road ahead, to the boy between coat and eiderdown, Zalman trilled, 'Paze-e-e-e-er!'

★

THE NIGHT Zalman set out to retrieve the boy Mila tossed in bed. Her agitation grew when Zalman did not return the following evening. The same fear kept awakening her. 'What if they were caught?'

Atara tried to reassure her, the war was over and Zalman expected the trip to last a few days, especially if, at first, the boy did not wish to leave.

'Your father is stubborn,' Mila said. 'The boy will have to come.' She did not voice her confusion about whether it was right to take the boy away from his new mother.

The two girls were leaning over the balcony's railing, eyes searching the road to Deseu, when the cart turned the corner.

'They're here!'

They rushed down the stairs: Mila, Atara, Hannah, and the younger children.

Hannah welcomed the boy exuberantly, 'Shulem Aleichem!' She lifted the eiderdown from his arms, insisted that he wanted something to drink, to eat.

The Stern children marvelled that a farm boy could be standing in their entranceway. Zalman's big, black skullcap looked odd on the boy's shoulder-length, honey-coloured hair. His face was tanned, not like the indoor complexion of yeshiva boys. While the other children escorted him into the kitchen where Hannah readied a meal for him, Mila slipped away. The boy had not caught sight of her; Mila knew better than to add that encounter to the strangeness that surrounded him. Sitting on the bed in the girls' room, her face held a relief not seen during the two years she had been with the Sterns. She rose, turned eastward, and prayed for the messiah with renewed fervour; surely this first reunion with Josef was a sign of the reunion to come when her parents would live again.

Zalman whisked the boy to synagogue for evening service.

Mila and Atara were in bed when they heard Zalman chant in the stairwell, and the key in the front door. Mila listened for the boy's footsteps and her body turned as she tracked him around the house. 'He recognises it from when he was little, the smell of chicken soup and the smell of starched Sabbath clothes. He hears the plop-pof of your mother's fists kneading the challah dough. He knows the quiet part when she removes the sticky paste from between her fingers.' Mila rose out of bed and pressed her ear against the door. 'He is going to the kitchen but it isn't his mother. It isn't either of his mothers.'

In the morning, Zalman called from the study: 'Hannah, is Josef up? Make sure he rises properly.'

Hannah coached the boy: '*I give thanks before Thee for returning my soul* . . . You didn't wash your hands before getting out of bed? How will your soul know that you are ready for it? When you are asleep, your soul rushes up near its Creator and, without a soul, your body becomes impure. Take hold of the cup with your right hand, good, now switch it to the left. Pour the water over the right hand. Switch the cup back; pour it over the left. Now repeat after me, *Blessed art Thou Adonaï* . . .'

Hannah set in front of the boy a glass of milk, two slices of buttered bread topped by two slices of tomato sprinkled with salt. '*Blessed art Thou Adonaï* . . . Now eat, Gutten Appetit.'

In between oven and baking board, Hannah turned the pages of little Etti's aleph-beth.

Etti pointed her chubby finger to the black letter. 'Aleph!'

'Josef, surely you remember your aleph-beth?' Hannah said.

The boy stared at the pink ribbon in Etti's hair. He pushed back his chair, walked out of the kitchen, to the front door.

Zalman called from the study: 'He went outside before saying grace?'

'Don't push the child,' Hannah said.

'You call obeying God's command pushing a child?'

Josef was banging his foot against the stone stairs in the courtyard.

'A Jewish boy doesn't stand idle,' Zalman called from the window. 'Come inside.'

The boy did not budge.

It was then that Mila hurried down the stairs and stopped a few treads above him.

'Anghel? It's me, Mila.'

He took a slow step towards her. He blinked. She turned on her heels. He followed her up the stairs.

During the Sabbath meal, when Zalman handed him a slice of challah, the boy thanked him in Romanian, 'Mulţumesc.'

'One speaks Yiddish at the Sabbath table. Yiddish is the language God considers his own,' Zalman coached.

Between courses, Josef stashed a challah bun into his pocket.

'The poor boy must have gone hungry,' Hannah whispered in the kitchen when the girls cleared the table.

In bed, in the dark, Mila whispered to Atara, 'The bun is not for him, it's for Florina.'

Sunday, Josef argued behind the closed door of Zalman's study. 'What does she tell the field hands? What does she say happened to me? Who was I?'

'The Eibershter will reward Doamna Florina a thousandfold, in this world and the next. I will also see to it, she will not lack a thing. As for you, our people in America are moving Heaven and earth. It won't be long before your affidavit arrives.'

'I don't want to go to America. I don't need to. Florina baptised me.'

Zalman leapt out of his seat. He struggled to take hold of himself. He leaned forward. His nose almost touching the Talmud tome, he inhaled deeply. When he lifted his face, it was serene again. 'The Rebbe is planning a holy community in America. He is asking for you.'

'If I plough the big fields in America, I can bring Florina?'

'A boy your age thinks of Torah study, not of ploughs and fields.'

'I will not see Florina again?'

'Only the Riboïne shel Oïlem knows such things.'

'What's Riboïne shel Oïlem?'

'Why — the Master of the Universe Who saved you once and Who will save you again by returning you to a world of Torah. Be grateful, Josef Lichtenstein. In time, you will send the woman money, parcels. You'll send her coffee, sugar, but a boy your age belongs in yeshiva. Only Torah study will bring the messiah and only the messiah will return our dead — yes, yes, our martyred ones will live again.'

'My mother, father, Pearela?'

'They will rise whole as if nothing happened. The Trumpets will sound. At the first blast, the world will shake. At the second blast, the dust will break up. The bones will gather at the third blast.' Taking in the boy's wide-open eyes, Zalman smiled. 'Your great-granduncle Reb Elimelech was a renowned Torah scholar. People travelled days just to glimpse at him, and you, too, can grow into a ben Torah; you, too, can hasten the coming of the messiah, Josef, son of Yekutiel and Judith.'

'Anghel.'

'Forget Anghel. Anghel is a name of fear. A Jew who fears God need not fear the Goyim. Be grateful, Josef Lichtenstein, our Lord saved you once and then He saved you again by bringing you back into His fold.'

Curled under the eiderdown, Josef clutched its faded tassels and chased his memories. 'Be grateful . . .'

He hadn't thought of telling Florina when she whispered, *Mama wants Anghel to live* . . . Every night, hands nestled between her hands, feet between her calves, he had clung to the sound of Florina's breath, but he hadn't thought of telling her that he was grateful.

Zalman informed the family that there was no time to waste in getting Josef ready for his bar mitzvah. Every morning, he took the boy into his study. Mila and Atara could hear, behind the closed door, Josef's thin, startled voice repeating the name of each cantillation, and Zalman coaching: 'In the holy tongue, cantillation signs are called *taamim*, which also means *flavours*. These little flourishes above and below the letters not only score the melody of the text, they bring out its essence. In time you, too, will savour the holy verses.'

The boy's uncertain voice chanted after Zalman: 'Kadma-ah munah zarka-a-a-ah . . .'

Zalman bellowed: 'Let your voice rise, come out of hiding, Josef, son of Yekutiel!'

In Josef's sleep, the black-limbed curlicues scuffled and spun threads he could not unravel, Zalman stories within Christ stories amid which Josef searched for a last letter, a first letter, that spelled a lost word . . .

THE WEEK BEFORE the High Holy Days, Zalman sat an uneasy Josef on a chair placed on top of unfolded newspapers and called for the children. He untied a knot above his ear and let down a thick dark curl. 'The Lord tells us, *You shall not round the corners of your heads.*' Then, picking up a razor, he said to Josef: 'You, too, must wear God's mark if you want Him to recognise you as His own. In Egypt, Jews maintained their traditions; they did not adapt dress, language, or names, and the Lord recognised them and took them out of bondage.'

The boy's hair fell on the newspapers as Zalman shaved him to the scalp, leaving two sidecurls.

That night, Mila and Atara heard the boy steal down the stairs. From their open window, they saw him run down the dimly lit street, to the church at the end of the block. They watched him huddle against the dark portal that so disquieted the girls.

Later, lying in bed, they heard a thin, continuous wail.

They held their breaths. The wail persisted. Mila rose. Her bare feet fluttered on the parquet as she left the room. The wail stopped.

Mila held the boy's shorn head between her arms, pressed it against her heart, warmed him with her whispers: '*Shayfeleh … Shayfeleh …*'

THE DAYS OF AWE came. In Zalman's modest synagogue in the ancient city of Sibiu / Nagyszeben / Hermannstadt, they gathered: survivors from Transylvania Bukovina Galicia, and Slovakia Bohemia Moravia, and Podolia Volhynia Silesia … They rounded one another up, Jews who wished they could forget they were Jews and thin bent shadows who knew someone would remember; Jews who spoke no Romanian; Jews who spoke only Romanian.

Zalman's voice rose and they pressed forward. From the front pews to the last standing row, in the men's section downstairs, in the women's balcony, on the stairs leading to the vestibules, they thrust towards the raised platform where Zalman pleaded in his white robe that Jews, this year, be inscribed in the Book of Life.

And some of the sobs were asking not forgiveness but redress, as Zalman's voice billowed, *El maleh rachamim … God full of compassion …*

During the service for the dead, children with parents slipped past the tears and skipped outside the synagogue. If, by accident, an unorphaned toddler was found inside, caught between grown-up legs, a cry went up, as if evening a score: 'Let this child out, this child is not a mourner!' Atara and the younger siblings played in the courtyard during the service for the dead, but Mila and Josef stood within.

And Josef recognised the chant Zalman had sung by the graves, *El maleh rachamim* ... In Zalman's synagogue, it was not silent furrows that met the boy's loss, not harvesters leaning on hayforks, jeering at Florina's bastard, but wails and incantations to turn absence into meaning. In Zalman's synagogue, everyone wept with the boy as he remembered the smell of woollen prayer shawls and yellowing books in his father's pew.

And the boy sensed that part of him longed for the name that was his when he had mother, father, sister. Like Zalman at the lectern, he, Josef Lichtenstein, wanted the lost world to live again.

A few weeks later, Josef's papers arrived.

THE ENTIRE FAMILY accompanied Josef to the station; Zalman, Hannah with the new baby pressed to her bosom, Mila and the Stern children holding hands.

The train doors clicked shut. Josef reappeared at a window, half hidden by the eiderdown. His face was still tanned but it looked bare, fragile, without the frame of hair.

Pipes gasped. The train started to roll.

Josef's eyes were fixed on Mila, on her plaits flying about her face as she ran to keep up with his car.

The train faded to a dot, vanished. Arms limp at her sides, Mila stood at the far edge of the platform, above the bed of cracked stone.

Book II

Autumn 1947

ZALMAN GATHERED THE FAMILY IN HIS STUDY. THE Talmud tomes that ordinarily lay open on his desk were wrapped in cloth. 'Children, you have come to think of Sibiu as your home, but until the Almighty delivers us from exile, we Jews have no home.' He lifted a stack of folios and placed them in a wooden crate. 'The government is closing down our schools, the communists – let their names be erased – want you to forget you are Jews. A small congregation in Paris needs a cantor. We are leaving.'

Mila and Atara looked up in surprise. They had heard Zalman yearn for the great yeshiva towns of Pressburg, Slobodka, Lezhinsk – never for *Paris*. Mila reached for Atara's hand, relieved that if they were to go, they would be going together.

The children were not to be sad, there had been far worse partings; nor were they to delight in being condemned to wander. When their playmate Marika called from the yard, Hannah warned that there was no time for games or farewells. The children heard Marika's pebble strike the cobbles, and her count as she hopped over the chalk lines. They listened to her silence as she picked up the marker. 'Atara, Mila, I won!'

One last morning, Mila and Atara woke in their shared bed. They listened to the swallows' twitter under the eave. They helped carry the cardboard suitcases and cloth bundles, helped load the horse cart.

Hugging the baby to her chest, Hannah climbed on top of the luggage, on top of the flatbed. Zalman lifted the toddlers and placed them next to her. Mila and Atara followed the cart on foot. Behind them walked Zalman and the eldest boy, five-year-old Schlomo.

Marika jumped rope beside the girls until the cart turned the corner. 'You're not coming back? Ever?' She stood at the corner, hopping from foot to foot and calling after them, 'Ever-ever?'

Mila and Atara helped load the bundles and suitcases onto the train. The family settled into a compartment. The train pulled out of the station. The weathercock on the copper dome flew away. The clock tower shrunk out of sight. Apartment blocks gave way to cottages, to thatched huts, to kerchiefed women tilling vegetable patches. The children waved to the women, to the horse harnessed to a lumber cart, to cheese bags tied to porch beams, to the southern Carpathians, to nightfall on the Cibin.

Darkness rattled past the window. The baby whimpered and Hannah placed him at her breast. The suckle filled the compartment. Atara leaned her head against Mila's shoulder and Mila leaned her head against Atara's head. The girls, who so wanted to stay awake for every moment of the journey, were soon rocked to sleep.

'The hen! It's running from the train!' Mila cried out.

Hannah leaned towards the girls. 'Shh, it's a dream, only a dream.'

'The hen doesn't want to die!' Mila protested.

'Shh, you'll wake the baby.'

Atara whispered into Mila's ear, 'We're safe. We're on a *passenger* train, we're going to Paris to live.'

Mila whispered back, 'Do *you* believe I saw the Rebbe on the train?' Her tone was urgent, as if she feared her memories, too, might be left behind.

Atara hesitated. 'But if the Rebbe was there, how come there was no miracle?'

Mila pulled away and leaned her head against the window. 'I *saw* him. He was wearing a white coat. He never looked up from his book but I saw him.'

Mila fell back asleep. Her head bounced against the rattling pane. Atara tilted Mila, gently, until Mila's head came to rest on Atara's shoulder. Atara listened to the compartment's door clicking in and out of its socket: her first sliding door, her first blue bulb casting shadows on Zalman's beard, and everything she would encounter now would be a first, the conductor's strange accent – she looked to Zalman to make sure he had not noticed her excitement, she looked into the speeding night.

They changed trains in Oradea and Budapest; they crossed the Austro-Hungarian border, which, a few months later, would shut for forty years. They changed trains in Vienna. As the stations went by – Linz, Munich, Stuttgart – cities, towns, villages emptied of Jews, Zalman and Hannah recited psalms that streaked their cheeks.

Paris

THE STERNS MOVED INTO A FOURTH-FLOOR APARTMENT
on the rue de Sévigné, in the Marais, the Jewish quarter.
Mila and Atara still shared a room but now had separate
beds. Their first night apart, they placed a chair between
the two brass frames for their joined hands to rest on, so
they would not uncouple in sleep.

'Françoise!' a voice called across the courtyard and the
girls' fingers gripped as they sounded the new vowels,
'Fran-çoise,' and once again they practised their new
address in the *qua-tri-ème ar-ron-dis-sement* . . .

Sound by sound, the neighbourhood fell asleep. The
girls, too, were drifting off when they heard Zalman
leave the master bedroom. Rather than settle into his
study, as he would many nights in Sibiu, Zalman walked
down the long hallway stacked with moving crates. The
kitchen door scraped open and closed.

Swish, the blade skimmed the whetstone, swish swish
. . . a high-pitched blade for circumcision, and lower-
pitched ones for animal slaughter . . . swish . . . swish . . .

The girls squeezed each other's hands, to see if the
other was hearing. Zalman was sharpening his ritual
knives by the kitchen sink. Surely this was not something

the Law asked of him, not right away, not in the middle of the night. It must have been Zalman himself who needed to do this. Swish . . . swish . . . the knives accelerated and he breathed intently . . . or was it their own breaths the girls were hearing?

The sounds stopped. Zalman retraced his steps along the crates. A drawer in his secretaire slid open, then the key of the secretaire turned in its lock, and the girls' hands, heavy with sleep, let go of each other.

Swallows singing new French songs woke them. Atara opened the window. Mila leaned into the light as it poured down silver roofs and cast ringlets of shade on peeling shutters. The younger children's laughter in the next room almost drowned out the bolt of the front door clicking open and shut; Zalman leaving for morning services. The girls tiptoed past the dining room where the flowered oilcloth still released its travel folds, they tiptoed into the master bedroom and climbed into Hannah's bed. Soon the younger children scurried in and they all snuggled against Hannah: Mila, Atara, Schlomo, the two toddlers, and Hannah's bed was a wide, white barge, her eiderdown a sail that steered them through the foreign morning.

A bead of light filtered between the shutter's slats and came to rest on Hannah's night cap. Little Etti tried to lift the pearl of light between thumb and index. Hannah laughed. When the baby whimpered in his crib, Hannah said, 'Milenka, my eldest, will you know how to carry, carefully, little Mendel Wolf?' Mila leapt out of bed, leaned over the crib, lifted the baby. Hannah unbuttoned the top of her night shift. The children watched the tiny fists closing on Hannah's breast, the tiny, avid lips; once more, they settled in their warm hollows.

Zalman returned from services and Hannah hurried out

of the room. Zalman sighed as he placed his black hat on the coat rack. Lingering in the warmth of Hannah's bed, the children heard the note of anguish in his voice. He told Hannah about the congregation: Would there be anyone with whom Zalman would share again the passion of Torah study he had shared with Mila's father? How far they had come from the Rebbe's court – there a Jew felt alive!

At breakfast, still perplexed by the new French bread, Schlomo insisted every hole in his slice be *filled* with butter. 'Please, Atara, this one too! It's looking at me—'

Zalman entered the room; Schlomo fell silent. Zalman took his seat at the head of the table and sighed.

Schlomo watched the butter sink downward into his bread. He reached for the knife, trying to spread even more onto the slice. Giving up on the knife, he scooped the butter with a finger and squashed it into a hole. Atara suppressed a giggle. Schlomo looked up, reproachfully.

Zalman's fist thumped the table.

'Goyim can't control their bodily inclinations but a Jew thinks of God's will only!'

The children stilled.

Zalman turned to his eldest son. 'Nu? When the Lord tells Israel *You shall be a holy nation*, what does *holy* mean?'

'*Separate*,' Schlomo replied. 'It is written in the Midrash Rabbah that holy means separate.'

'Good. *You shall be a holy nation*, you shall set yourself apart. As we wander through this Parisian wilderness, remember: When we Jews behave like other nations, God punishes us.' His tone grew sharper. 'Surely the messiah should be here after all that we have endured, but some among us are holding the messiah back.'

Etti started to whimper.

'In the so-called Jewish school where, alas, I am sending you, you may hear − God forbid, you may hear − of a blasphemy that calls itself *Jewish Enlightenment*. But the Chassam Sofer says the Torah forbids innovation. You may hear of *Enlightenment*'s sinister offshoot: Zionism. Our Rebbe says Zionism was responsible for the terrible destruction. A Zionist army will protect us?' Zalman's fist slammed the table.

The milk in the children's bowls lifted in curls that collapsed over the rims and onto the oilcloth.

Etti burst into sobs.

Zalman's brow furrowed. His pulse galloped. It was essential for children to fear their father so they would grow into God-fearing Jews. His voice rose above the toddler's sobs.

'Who are we to stand up to the nations when God wills us to submit? Who are we to build a Jewish state when God decrees our exile? God made us swear three oaths.' Zalman turned to his eldest son. 'What is the first?'

Schlomo hesitated. Zalman scanned the other children's faces but they did not know.

'The first oath: That we will not storm the wall of exile. The second: That we will not rebel against the nations amongst whom we are exiled. The third: That we will not force the End.

'We must not build the Promised Land with our own strength. Our deliverance will come through wonders and miracles and whoever doubts this miraculous redemption doubts the entire Torah. May HaShem free us from the enemies that surround us, may He deliver us from exile, Amen.'

'Amen,' the children echoed.

Zalman rose and trod heavily towards the door.

THAT AFTERNOON, flying over the slide's hump in the Luxembourg Gardens, it was hard for the children to remember they were wandering in the desert; soaring in the boat-shaped swings, it was hard to remember they were chosen to set themselves apart. When the children did remember, they shrilled louder plummeting down the slide and tore back up as if this descent might be the last before they were gathered out of exile. Mothers on benches shook their heads. Surely this brood with sidecurls and long skirts was the loudest the Luxembourg had ever heard.

'Why so much joy in the wilderness?' Zalman reprimanded when the children clambered up the flights home, cheeks flushed with play. 'Where do you think the Jewish children are, who lived here before you? Which of our neighbours handed them over?'

In Sibiu, Zalman had tolerated that his sons toss marbles in the yard, but he no longer permitted it in Paris. 'Bitul z'man' (*waste of time*), he scolded the boys who followed him to his study, ears crimson from his angry clip. Girls were permitted to jump rope or play hopscotch when Hannah did not need help, but boys old enough to read were to sit in front of the holy books.

Mila and Atara could sense that Zalman, so valiant in the desolation of back there, was afraid of Paris. They wanted to reassure him. They vowed that their piety would console the ilui who had lost his world. At the close of the Sabbath, when women were not expected to attend services, they accompanied him to synagogue. Like Zalman, they stepped off the kerb to avoid coming near a place of idol worship, a church. Like him, they turned their eyes from the graven images that adorned façades and fountains – had God saved their bodies so their souls might perish? Zalman seized the girls' hands before crossing the street, that is, he wrapped his palms around their wrists, slowed them with a tighter clasp. Zalman touched his children so rarely that his firm hold circling their wrists filled the girls with an exquisite sense of protectedness. Sometimes Zalman forgot to let go when they reached the opposite pavement and then it did not matter if people stared and knew he was their father, the Jew with the untrimmed beard who would not shake women's hands; it did not matter if someone snickered *sales juifs*, dirty Jews. Zalman leaned towards the girls. 'The same clothes that point us out to the hatred of the Goyim also point us out to Him who dwells in Heaven.'

Swish . . . the knives skimmed the whetstone.

Swish . . . the girls' skipping rope whisked the corridor's floorboards.

Zalman stepped out of the kitchen, the blades' gleam secure behind felt cloth. Pressed against the wallpaper, Mila and Atara knew not to upset his course. When the door of his study closed, their skipping resumed, solemn, as the ancient desert threat cast its shadow and flew past.

THE CHILDREN were in the entryway, preparing to leave for their first day of school, when Zalman emerged from his study. The girls bit their lips, afraid to be late.

'You will watch over yourselves,' he instructed, 'and you will watch over one another. If the puppets of Satan gather to celebrate their new mirage, their *State* of Israel, you will stand apart, separate. Blimela, you are the eldest' – Zalman always called Mila by her Yiddish name – 'you will watch over the younger ones.' Mila nodded. 'Remember, Blimela, when you observe HaShem's commandments, your parents' souls, up there, come nearer to His presence, but when you stray, they are banished to a cold desert where souls freeze and shatter.'

Mila closed her eyes to better see her parents depending on her for warmth.

'The children will be late,' Hannah whispered to Zalman.

'The Lord is giving us one more chance. May He free us from the enemies that surround us, may He deliver us from exile, Amen.'

'Amen,' the children echoed, adjusting the shoulder straps of their schoolbags.

The bell was ringing when they entered the yard. Mila and Atara dropped off their younger siblings with the nursery-school teacher and ran to join the line already disappearing into the main building. They marvelled at being in the same grade even though Mila was almost one year older and had finished first grade in Sibiu, but Zalman could obtain only one segregated class; the school of heretics permitted that boys and girls study together.

Tall windows took up one wall of the bright room. The teacher stood in front of a lined blackboard; she was pretty even though she wore trousers. They must not tell Zalman about the trousers. Children's paintings of blue stars on white paper were taped in a continuous frieze on the remaining two walls.

Mila and Atara were shown two empty desks in the back of the room. Some of the children turned their heads and smiled, others leaned close together and whispered.

Every morning, the girls' eyes shone when they opened their *cahiers d'école*, notebooks with pages white, smooth, ruled and cross-ruled by pale blue lines. They dipped their new pens into the glass inkwell, how lovely it was to trace, meticulously, the new French words, the ascenders and descenders.

THE TEACHER announced there would be a celebration of Israel's Declaration of Independence. Mila looked up, to the frieze of blue stars. Her nib caught and scratched the paper, spitting a drop of ink on the white page. Once again, the two girls would be set apart. Mila flushed when she remembered that three times already Atara and she had been the designated robbers during break time. Their classmates' war cries encircled them, and Atara and she cowered against each other, then fled inside the building where pupils were not allowed during break time. The pretty teacher came down the stairs in her trousers. Atara and Mila lowered their eyes, ashamed to tell that their classmates ganged up on them. The teacher looked at them lengthily, at their long skirts, their thick stockings. She asked whether it was true that their father would not permit them to study for the *baccalauréat*, later. The girls answered they did not know, they did not know what the *bacca* – what it was.

Atara stared at the spot of ink on Mila's page.

Mila whispered, 'We must find out when the celebration will take place.'

'Quiet!' the teacher called.

If they could find out the exact day, surely Zalman and Hannah would let them stay home – Zalman would *want* them to stay home.

THE BLUE Star of David fluttered in the bright May sky, above the classes assembled in the schoolyard. At a second-floor window, holding a megaphone, the principal gave an impassioned speech: There were lessons surviving Jews *must* learn from history and one such lesson was that powerlessness was not an option. The euphoric voice bounced out of the Zionist megaphone. 'No longer *next* year but *this* year – *this* year in our new State of Israel!'

The yard roared. Teachers and students joined hands. A classmate reached for Atara's hand, to invite the two girls in the giant round, but Mila and Atara shook their heads and pressed harder into the back wall, to meld into it, even as their eyes did not lift from the linked hands and stamping feet, even as their ears could not help but learn the most prohibited of songs: *Our hope is not yet lost, to be a free nation in our land . . .*

But boys and girls holding hands, singing together, dancing together, celebrating the End when the End had not come – all of it was forbidden.

63

Walking home, Mila and Atara were silent. All week, Mila could not look Zalman in the eyes. She begged God to examine her heart and see that she had not intended to force the End. She, Mila Heller, would wait, patiently, to be saved.

*

HANNAH AND ZALMAN hired Leah Bloch, a nineteen-year-old seminary graduate, to foil the traps of the impious école and give the girls additional instruction on modesty and religious observance. Pale, thin-lipped Leah Bloch, who fantasised that the new Hasidic family from afar was hers, instead of her own ordinary French family, explained that Mila and Atara must be proud of their lineage, of parents who were not dupes of the French *lumières*. She taught the girls to read Scripture the proper way – never the words of Scripture alone, but always accompanied by the revered commentators' interpretations. She sang fervent, pious songs to counter the songs the girls were hearing in school. Every Sabbath afternoon, Leah Bloch and the girls danced to the tune: *'I want the messiah, now!'*

Leah Bloch informed Hannah about Mila and Atara not partaking in the forbidden celebration. Zalman called the girls into his study. He looked at one then the other; he smiled. 'Nu?' Every afternoon that week, he taught them to sing in harmony a passage from the Days of Awe services, a difficult prayer tune he had been teaching the boys who would accompany him in synagogue, but Mila and Atara had fine voices even if they could not sing in public, not in front of men. Mila was not yet twelve so she could sing in front of Zalman despite not being his daughter.

★

EAGER TO ASSUME responsibilities beyond tutoring the girls, Leah Bloch ran errands for Hannah and took the children to the park. When Leah Bloch held the hands of the younger siblings, Mila and Atara could sprint ahead, over the arcing bridges, to the gold-tipped arrows of the Luxembourg's gates.

And so it was that one radiant Sabbath afternoon, Mila and Atara entered the gardens alone. Giddy leaves peeked out of every bud, on every tree.

The girls dashed forward.

'Aha!' the combed gravel let out.

The rusticated columns of the Palais du Luxembourg folded inside the pond's ripples, swirled around the fountain, vanished into droplets of water-sun—

'Atara! Mila!'

Across the terrace, straddling her bicycle, the girls' new playground friend, Nathalie, waved. 'You want it for a lap?' she yelled.

Mila and Atara ran to the bicycle. Mila straddled the frame; Atara perched on the rear rack.

'One lap only!' Nathalie called after them.

Mila's right foot weighed down on the pedal, the left foot weighed down. The spokes cast their spinning shadows as the bike overtook the toy sails in the pond. Mila leaned into a curve; Atara clasped Mila's waist. Mila pedalled faster; Atara's arms flew up. Mila slowed by the sandpit where toddlers rapped each other's heads with plastic spades – on a bicycle, even decelerating was a thrill. Mila's shoe slipped on the pedal and the bicycle tipped to one side; Atara leaned to the other side and the bike regained its enchanted balance.

The other shoe slipped on the pedal, the leather sole of Mila's black patent Sabbath shoe—

Surely there had been no bicycles on Mount Sinai, Atara thought. Had there been one, then riding it would never have been forbidden on the day of rest, because it wasn't work at all and one was meant to rejoice on the Sabbath— 'My turn now!' Atara called.

Mila slowed and the girls switched positions. Atara stood up on the pedals. Flowers and hedges blurred past as she accelerated. Children's cries speckled the air, soared with the swings, bounced on the slide's hump—

A shriek.

Tearing across the lawn, Leah Bloch, followed by the toddlers.

Atara braked. The back wheel skidded.

'Sabbath!' Leah Bloch screamed with all her might.

Mila and Atara tumbled off the bicycle before it fully stopped.

'You're still touching it!' Leah Bloch cried out.

Atara let go of the bike, which fell to the ground.

'Sabbath!' Leah Bloch let out again. 'You must tell your father, you must tell him what you did on the Sabbath.'

Mila remembered that if Jews kept *one* Sabbath only, if they kept one Sabbath perfectly, the messiah would come and her parents would live again. She wiped the tears from her cheeks.

Atara went to look for Nathalie while the bike lay on the gravel. Atara tried to explain: No, she had not fallen off the bike, no, neither Mila nor she was hurt, no, she could not bring the bike back – she could not *touch* it.

Mila and Atara left the Luxembourg through a gate they had not taken before. Would Zalman find out?

67

Someone from the congregation might have seen the new rabbi's children transgressing the Sabbath ... Would Leah Bloch tell? A sibling? The girls wandered along the quays, far, until hoarse seagull calls carved the setting sun. They reasoned that eight and seven was too young to run away. Hair bows limp to the sides of their faces, they began to retrace their steps.

Perhaps if Zalman saw them first in the synagogue, he would be less angry?

The girls lingered between the pews of the unlit women's balcony.

Soon Zalman stood in the doorway; Zalman would not enter the balcony even though no grown woman was there. He signalled to the girls. They advanced. Atara was closest to him; one spank sent her flying down the vestibule's three steps. 'Go home!'

Zalman had never spanked his children.

The girls made their way home.

Hannah turned from them.

In their Sabbath dark room — it was forbidden to flick a switch and turn on a light on the Sabbath — the girls sat on the same bed.

Zalman came back from evening services sombre, intent. He lit the plaited candle, poured wine to the brim of the silver goblet — to inherit this world and the next.

'Where are they, the transgressors of the Sabbath?' he asked.

'In their room,' a child whispered.

'Go fetch them. A God-fearing Jew is obligated to hear Havdala.'

The girls appeared, gazes cast down. Zalman intoned the prayer that separates Sabbath from weekday, sacred from profane. When he finished, the room was silent.

Mila started for the kitchen, for the sink full of dirty Sabbath dishes.

'Stay!' Zalman commanded.

He slid off his belt.

Mila froze in the doorway.

Atara plunged under the daybed.

Zalman pulled the bed from the wall.

Atara swerved to maintain cover.

The bed jerked right, left; Atara ducked right, left.

The bed lurched and seesawed and Zalman grew angrier.

'You're only making matters worse! Get out of there!'

Atara stilled. Zalman's hand reached for her, his yad chazakah moulded on God's own mighty hand. He dragged the girl out, bent her over his knee, pulled down her pyjamas.

Even toddlers did not crawl naked in Zalman's house.

'My child mocks God's word in public?'

The belt lashed the air and Atara's buttocks. Her legs wriggled, trying to escape, but her feet did not reach the ground.

'A profaner of the Sabbath – a man who gathers sticks on the Sabbath, all the congregation shall stone him!'

Mila shuddered with each blow.

'Stop, Tatta, stop!' the children sobbed.

'The rebellious son, his parents must do the stoning.'

Belt belt belt.

'I will instil fear of Heaven in my children.'

Belt. Belt. Belt.

'Zalman! Isn't it enough?' Hannah pleaded.

'Do not intervene! I will break secularism.' Belt. 'Zionism.' Belt. 'Modernity.' Belt.

Atara was no longer screaming.

'Repeat after me: Never again will I transgress the

69

Sabbath, not the Sabbath nor any of the Lord's Holy Days.'

The girl hiccuped the commanded words.

Zalman let go of her.

She slid under the daybed. Zalman rose and took a step towards Mila, coiled belt in hand. Anger dented and swelled his forehead.

He saw the spreading stain on Mila's white tights and the puddle around her shoes, widening. His head turned away. His raised arm dropped to his side.

He stopped in the doorway. 'You have disobeyed the Lord and you have shamed me, deeply. You have shamed the family. Now the apikorsim (*nonbelievers*) mock: Here goes the pious Hasid whose children transgress the Sabbath.'

Zalman left the room. In his study, head in his hands, he recited the texts affirming what he had done.

'SHUSH NOW!' Hannah said, wiping the toddlers' noses. In the next room, the baby squealed. Hannah looked at the puddle at Mila's feet, she hesitated. 'Go and wash, then take the younger children to bed.' The children gripped Hannah's dress. The baby's shrieks grew louder. Hannah pulled away but the children held on as she started for the door. She leaned over the crib, lifted the baby, paced back and forth with the baby in her arms; the sobbing children followed her back and forth. 'Quiet!' Hannah said. 'Your father and I are trying to protect you— Mila,' she called to the next room, 'get a hold of yourself. I need your help.' Hannah leaned sideways and wiped more noses. 'It's important to watch over one another, to shield one another from sin. It's important not to encourage wicked-ness – the baby is *hungry*, let go of my dress. No one will punish *you* if you say *no* to your evil inclination. Mila! Now, I need help *now*! Put the children to bed and say HaMapil with them. I'll see to Atara.'

The children held on to Mila's hands and followed her to their room. They climbed into the same bed.

'Talk to us,' Etti whined.

'At-Atara!' Schlomo stammered.

'Can you hear us, Mila?' Etti asked. 'No, she doesn't hear us.'

Little Etti's hand stroked Mila's shoulder. 'Please Mila, Mama said you must say HaMapil with us, *Lay me to sleep in peace and wake me* . . . Mila? Mila, look at Schlomo!'

The boy's face twitched.

Mila's hand came to his cheek. 'When my parents live again they'll take care of us.'

'I don't like Tatta,' Etti said.

'Halilah, you mustn't say that!' Mila shot out. 'You must *honour* Father and Mother.'

'Atara . . .' Schlomo whispered.

Etti and the toddlers started to sob again.

The children heard Hannah's step outside, entering the dining room, and they fell silent. Her ear pressed to the door, Mila held her breath.

'Atara, are you still under there?' they heard Hannah ask. 'You can come out, the other children are in bed . . . Atara?'

When there was no reply, Etti started: '*Michael is to my right, Gabriel to my left, Uriel is in front . . . Raphael . . . Above is the Presence of the Lord. Michael is . . .*'

In the dining room, Hannah sat at the table, a few feet from Atara under the daybed. Her weary eyes closed. The teething infant had cried all afternoon.

'Atara, your father, he was only . . . Do you hear me?'

Silence.

Hannah gazed at her open Book of Psalms but her lips whispered another prayer, that the Lord remember her exile, she too an orphan, may the Lord remember Hannah-Leah, daughter of Zissel-Malkah, she who was so tired, and Zalman so lost and angry in this Paris of lights, may the Lord shield the children from temptation—

'Atara?'

Hoping Atara's stillness was sleep, desperate to fall into bed while the baby was quiet, Hannah turned off the light and left the room.

The door shut.

There, under the daybed, in darkness cramped with shame, pain, and chattering teeth, a seed pierced through, a seed as vigorous as Zalman's belt-swinging arm, a seed rising to the commandment scored on her buttocks as on two stones: If God cared that Atara Stern rode a bicycle on the Sabbath, then Atara Stern did not care for—

'Atara! It's me.' Mila's hand tapped the floor under the bed. 'It's me, Mila. It's going to be all right, please come out.'

Silence.

'Please,' Mila whimpered, 'it's me.' Mila stooped down and looked into the dark under the daybed.

Atara rolled closer to the wall. 'Go away.'

'Atara . . .' Mila called now and again, and waited.

Eventually Atara slid out from under the bed and they stood facing each other in the moonlight that fell across the parquet. They lowered their eyes.

'I'm sorry,' Mila whispered, 'I also rode Nathalie's bicycle, I also committed the sin. But he'll still come, Atara, the messiah will come and my parents will live again and you and I—'

Atara, who had prayed every evening for the messiah to bring Mila's parents back to life, heard herself proclaim: 'Dead people do not live again.' Then Atara moved past Mila — past Mila's need — and holding back tears, walked herself out of the room.

Mila clutched the table as she listened to Atara's receding footsteps.

'*Michael is to my right, Gabriel to my left ... Uriel in front ... HaShem ...* HaShem, I won't ride a bicycle even on weekdays ... HaShem?'

A shadow plunged down the windowpane, Mila held her breath. Was her prayer falling backward? Was the room packed with wingless prayers that could not fly to Heaven and tumbled upon each other, dead?

★

NOW THAT HaShem was angry with her, Mila did not recite her prayers by rote, nor did she mix in her own words. Leah Bloch had explained that rabbis had weighed every letter in the prayer book to inspire sincere prayer, and God listened more carefully if one prayed in Hebrew even when one did not understand all the words.

Mila's eyes fixed the black ciphers, but her ears tracked each of Atara's movements. The toddlers ran rings around her, trying not to bump into Mila's house of whisperings. When Mila's eyes met the line indicating End of Morning Service, she brought the open page to her face and kissed the frayed prayer that affirmed her parents *would* live again.

During the day, she clung to the ancient rites of separation: Sabbath, weekday; sacred, profane; pure, impure. She shined and buffed all surfaces; she folded her undergarments into perfect squares, and to improve the odds that Atara would be with her when her parents returned, she disentangled the clump of undergarments in Atara's drawer and transformed it into perfect squares.

At night, the girls lay in their two beds, but the chair between them sat empty of hands. Mila stared into the dark, afraid of the bad dream: her mother shot, her father dragged across the rails ... Sometimes, when Mila had been a good Jew, she dreamt the good dream, in which her mother called *'Rebbe!'* and the Rebbe looked up from his book and sprang to his feet signalling them to hurry and they climbed into the open boxcar: her mama with her big belly, she in her tatta's arms, and when the train started again, they were all going where the Rebbe was going. But after the good dream, too, Mila would weep because it was only a dream. Atara would console her: 'Best friends, sisters for life.'

Now Atara was silent. 'Speak to me,' Mila murmured in the dark, but not loud enough to be heard.

On their way to Sunday school, Atara hurried ahead of Mila. She stopped on the bridge's crest. Her palms cupped the railing, her knee edged between two uprights. 'Wait for me, wait for me . . .' she whispered, her gaze racing with the current.

'Rivers don't care,' Mila said when she caught up with Atara.

'My river cares.'

★

On the Sabbath, Leah Bloch arrived to take the children to the park but Atara would not go. In the girls' room, the sun played on the freshly laid, spackled linoleum but Atara reached for the dog-eared book left at the bottom of a crate of toys the community had gathered for the new rabbi's children.

'You can't read a Goyish book on the Sabbath,' Mila whispered.

Atara turned the first page and scrutinised the illustration. She tried out the new French words: *'Ca-nard, jau-nes, oeufs . . .'*

'Please, Atara, be careful.'

Atara kept turning the pages. 'I think you'd like the story.'

Instead of protesting that she would not like a Goyish story, certainly not on the Sabbath, Mila said, 'I can sit next to you?'

Atara slid towards the wall to make room for Mila on her bed and continued to leaf through the illustrations.

A mother duck lining up her happy yellow ducklings. A big grey egg, opening. White swans gliding on top of their reflections. Staring at the last page, Atara said, 'The mother duck is here and the yellow ducklings are here and the swans are here, but where is the grey duckling?'

'Hiding? Behind the tree?'

'The grey duckling is hiding. He comes out at dark, when the swans sway their long necks and wave the day goodbye and when the swans tuck their bills under each other's wings, the duckling nestles in there too, like you and me they sleep on the dark lake—'

'But we are Jews,' Mila said.

'So?'

'Jews can't be ducks or swans.'

Atara pulled back the book. 'Yes they can!'

Revived by her Sabbath nap, Hannah took in the girls' laden silence. After Zalman left for evening services, she made them sit next to her, one on each side at her head of the table. Holding the girls' hands, Hannah sang: '*Oyfn veg, steyt a boym, shteyt er ayngeboygn—*' Hannah turned to Mila. 'Did your mama teach it to you – yes? Sing with me, Milenka.'

Mila joined in: '*Oy, Mama, I so want to be a bird and lullaby the tree through winter . . .*

'*Ah child, take your scarf, galoshes, fur hat, long underwear . . .*

'*Mama, my wings are heavy with so much love . . .*'

Hannah shot up, clasping the girls' hands, but Atara pulled away.

Hannah took Mila by the waist. '*Oy yadidadi yadidadi yadidadi, YADIDADIDAM!*' In the room filling with dusk as Queen Sabbath bowed her adieus, Hannah and Mila turned to the melancholy rhythm, to the old broken melody asking the young girls to bind up its wounds and carry it forward.

Hannah turned to Atara. 'Come, Ataraleh, dance!'

Atara pushed back her chair and clasped the doorknob.

Why were they singing *I so want to be a bird* the way they sang *I trust in the messiah's coming*? The bird song was different; it was about how she and Hannah felt, not how HaShem felt.

'Ataraleh!' Hannah called again.

Atara curled tighter at the foot of the door. The bird song was a trap, all of Hannah's songs were traps – Atara

77

wanted neither Hannah's Sabbath magic nor her weekday exhaustion.

FOUNTAIN NYMPHS and dolphin-straddling putti became the confidants for all the things Atara felt she could no longer tell Mila. Atara's hands reached for walls as if stones returned caresses, her lips whispered to crack and moss as if they whispered back. To the polished stones, Atara confided that one day, courage might call for a bigger self, not for making oneself smaller.

★

AT THE CAFÉ TERRACES sparrows skipped from marble tabletops to pavement, stubby beaks pecking the sun-swept cobbles. Crossing the church square on the way to Leah Bloch's Sunday class, the girls turned their heads to a loud voice: 'Here, Synagoga.' The girls' brows knitted in bafflement as their eyes followed the tour guide's finger pointing to the church portal, to the forbidden likeness, the stone maiden.

'Synagoga stands to the left of the Father, she looks away, blindfolded by a snake. Her staff is broken. The tables of the Law slip from her hand.'

The girls' gazes lingered on contrite Synagoga, her slim marble waist, her heavy chiselled hair, her tall fore-head cast down, forever in the wrong.

'To the Father's right,' the guide continued, 'crowned Ecclesia upholds the Redeemer's cross and His blood . . .'

Cameras clicked as the girls walked on, closer one to the other, through medieval lanes now vaguely threat-ening in their dominical silence.

That evening, Mila stood on her bed, nightgown cinched at the waist, a blindfold over her eyes. She giggled as a book slid from her hand. 'Whoohoo hoo am I?' Cheeks flushed, she jumped up and down on her bed. 'Whoohoohoo?'

Mila's giggle rippled through Atara, who climbed onto the bed. She, too, jumped up and down.

'To the Father's left!'

'Right!'

'Left!'

Mila jumped higher still. 'They hate me! Whoowhoo who am I?'

Spring 1952

MILA FOUND BLOOD BETWEEN HER THIGHS. HANNAH calmed her; there was no reason to be afraid, the blood was Eve's punishment for making Adam mortal. Mila learned a new prayer:

I receive with love this periodic chastisement. I would not have enjoyed the forbidden fruit...

Atara was not satisfied with Hannah's explanation. She decided to go to the forbidden public library and returned with a different explanation of Mila's blood, and with a book bag full of other stories.

Atara wanted to prefer Hannah's stories to the forbidden books. Hannah's stories started full of promise, with multi-coloured Yiddish words that Hannah did not speak in everyday life, but just when the bird was trembling on a winter branch, or the impoverished Torah scholar had met a spirit, the prayer words, and then HaShem himself, pushed their way in, and it seemed to Atara that Hannah's multicoloured words had been a ploy to introduce God words about punishing the wicked and rewarding those who feared. The evening when Atara realised that the lively words would *always* vanish from Hannah's stories, she stormed out of the room.

In the forbidden books, the coloured words sometimes continued inside her even after she had finished reading the story; then Atara wondered whether a secret passageway might link her to the outside world.

Soon Atara was reading all the time. She read on the way to school and back from school; she read under her desk in class; at night, she read by flashlight under her eiderdown.

In his study, Zalman swayed to the ancestral singsong of Talmudic disquisition; under her eiderdown, Atara read soundlessly, urgently. Only during Zalman's midnight lament over the Temples destroyed did his moan shear the lines off Atara's page. She raised her head, listened to his plea – waited for the shuffle of his slippers in the corridor. Silence? The words realigned themselves, once more drew her in.

Zalman's Talmud folios and Atara's books were like neighbours who share a building without knowing each other, except that now and then Zalman searched the girls' room for secular writings and tore them up. 'I will not raise a Spinoza, not under my roof!'

Always, Atara found a way. She slid the forbidden books between her belly and the waistband of her white underwear, she climbed on the wooden toilet seat and stashed the books on the outer sill of the high, narrow window.

Hannah was too busy with the younger children, too tired by her latest pregnancy, to watch over Atara's reading.

. . .

Mila peered at the ghostlike hump of eiderdown in Atara's bed. Just last year, the two girls still laughed with Leah Bloch at their poor grades in literature's trivialities, but now the teacher of literature called on Atara. Mila tried to remind Atara, timidly, that the books were forbidden, but Atara shot back that free will was a right in Judaism too; Atara's *free will* wanted to read books.

Leah Bloch reassured Mila: Atara's books were merely about pleasure, not serious matters. When you give in to forbidden desire, despair sets in, and emptiness; the secular world was full of mental illness. When Atara would be depressed and lonely, Mila would be there to save Atara.

Next to the glowing hump of eiderdown, Mila prayed: *'Michael is to our right, Gabriel to our left, Raphael...'*

At fourteen, Atara found her way to the Bibliothèque Sainte-Geneviève as if she had always known that such a space must exist and that she must be let in. In the hushed, tall reading room where lamps of milk glass inside green shells cast bright ellipses of light on rustling pages, she read contemporary authors. She did not read them in any order: One day she came across *Notre-Dame-des-Fleurs*, the next day she found *L'Être et le néant*. When words or concepts escaped her, she did not put the book aside; the more enigmatic the formulation, the richer the promise of freedom. When she left the library, pearly threads linked roof to roof, dormer to dormer, a luminescent web under which everyone was equally chosen.

She lingered in front of the Sorbonne, peeked into the

cobbled yard. The bell of the chapel rang. She darted through the crowd on the boulevard Saint-Michel, across the Seine, faster, to get home before Zalman noticed her absence.

WHEN MILA BEGAN TO MENTION CLASSES THAT
prepared for the *baccalauréat*, the diploma that opened
the doors to university, Zalman withdrew the girls
from the lycée. Mila and Atara were to help Hannah
around the house until they were of age to marry. Mila
was sixteen and Atara fifteen.

Hannah, however, remembered Leah Bloch praising
a highly reputed seminary for girls, in northern
England. Leah Bloch had spent her happiest years
there. Hannah was willing to forgo the help; a few
semesters of Torah study, away from house chores
and sibling care, would be Hannah's lasting gift to her
girls.

Zalman argued that the seminary, while ultra-
orthodox, was not run by Hasidim. Teaching Torah to
women was not the Hasidic way, nor was sending unmarried girls far from their father's guardianship. But the
thought of the two adolescent girls idle in Paris, and the
recurrent appearance of secular books in Atara's posses-
sion, troubled Zalman. He pondered recent rabbinic
rulings that saw no harm in women studying Scripture
and Ethics; he verified that there was no Talmud

instruction – which was expressly forbidden to women; he authorised the seminary.

A new urgency pervaded Atara's forays in the city; these August days might be the last she would call Paris home. After the seminary, she would be expected to marry abroad, in a Hasidic community. Zalman was adamant: not one of his children would settle in France; it was too hard to bring up Hasidic children in France. On the crest of the Pont Saint-Michel, Atara turned her head right, to Notre Dame's flying buttresses, to the forest of gargoyles and spires; she turned her head left, to the string of bridges arching over the Seine, the Pont Neuf, Pont des Arts . . . She loved the story of time the old stones told, time before her, after her, loved feeling herself to be a mere fleck in this immensity. The bells rang the hour, then the hour filled with silence and she filled with longing; must Paris be a mere way station on her wanderings? If Paris had a home in her heart, might she not have a home in Paris?

Atara day-dreamed of preparing for the *baccalauréat* with her classmates at the lycée, but then her family would be erased from the register of good Hasidic families, her siblings condemned to bad marriages, to no marriage at all . . . Was it a selfish heart that dreamt of living her own life?

THE TAXI'S HORN sounded through the open windows. The girls' suitcases sat on the landing. Hannah placed a finger on her lips and signalled the girls to follow her into the living room. She opened the dark walnut chest from Transylvania, now emptied except for two stacks of

86

new sheets and pillowcases. 'God willing, the chest will fill up, yes, your trousseaus. You are laughing, Milenka? Two, three years go by fast . . .'

Hannah kissed the girls, she blessed their journey: *'May the Lord bless you. May He guard your steps . . .'*

One last time, Zalman exhorted the girls to uphold the family's reputation and their Hasidic antecedents. *'May the Lord bless you. May He guard your steps . . .'*

★

THE TRAIN CLANKED its way north on the last leg of the long journey. Mila read her Book of Psalms; Atara stared out the window. *Northampton . . . Leicester . . . Nottingham.* Neither farmland nor city but vast stretches of humble brick houses, row after row of terraced houses punctuated by slag heaps and tall chimneys. *Doncaster . . . Newton Aycliffe.* Leah Bloch had challenged Atara; the most erudite rabbis taught at the seminary, some with broad knowledge not only in Torah matters but in worldly disciplines. If Atara applied herself, she would obtain answers to the questions she had not dared ask Zalman. It was urgent that Atara find answers that would ready her for marriage with the pious young man Zalman would find for her. *Stony Heap . . . Deaf Hill.* Atara made up her mind to try. She would study the holy texts as intently as she had read secular books. *No Place . . . Quaking Houses.* She would immerse herself in the seminary's teachings and perhaps the holy texts would work their magic on her, too; perhaps she would stop dreaming about the *baccalauréat* and learn to dream of preparing meals for the Sabbath so that Zalman's and Hannah's hearts would not break.

The carriage couplings clattered. The train crawled through hissing smoke and stopped under a dark vault.

Two girls in long skirts greeted Mila and Atara on the platform. In the taxi, the seminary girls talked excitedly about this year's entering class, the largest ever, forty-five, bless the Lord, almost a hundred in the entire seminary, the principal was very happy, bless the Lord, this year's T1 girls were all so special.

'T1 girls?' Atara asked.

'Teachers 1 – for Teacher's Training College, but the teacher's degree is granted only if one stays the entire three years.' The girl's voice held a note of regret.

'Marguit is engaged!' the second girl chimed in.

Mila and Atara shook Marguit's hand. 'Mazel tov!'

'Esti, too, is engaged!' Marguit teased.

'Mazel tov!'

The taxi stopped mid-block in front of a three-storey house. The older students explained that the seminary comprised four adjoining houses with interconnected corridors. No, Mila and Atara would not share the same room; all T1 girls were encouraged to make new friends.

SIX BEDS in two facing rows under a bare bulb. Cloth of faded green-and-wine corduroy screened six shelves. A loud bell, the bulb went out. The orange coil of the wall-mounted heater glowered and went dark. In the middle bed of the row facing the window, Atara pulled the coarse blanket to her nose. She would try; she must. She would learn to fall asleep without reading – where would she have hidden a book and a flashlight in a room shared with five girls? Lulling herself, she fell into the sensation that a train was rocking her to some farther destination, *tournent roues, tournent roues ... tournent ... tournent ...*

In the adjoining house, in a room with two facing rows of beds, Mila also lulled herself. Comforted by the fervour she sensed in the other girls whispering their bedtime prayers, she joined in: *'Michael is to my right, Gabriel to my left, Uriel is in front ...'*

Mila woke full of anticipation. She was thrilled to belong to the first generation of Hasidic women who would be studying Scripture. She looked forward to meeting girls from different walks of orthodox life: from Hasidic communities and Misnaged communities; from Litvak, Yekke, and Polish families; from every corner of Europe, from the two Americas, from Australia and South Africa – all in long skirts and long-sleeved blouses, girls among whom she would be, at last, normal.

The class schedule was: Pentateuch, Prophets, Midrash, Jewish Thought, Conduct. During Pentateuch class, Mila wondered: Had her father come across this very interpretation? Had gematriah enchanted him as it enchanted her? To Mila, gematriah felt occult yet cerebral, mystical yet rational, drawing the Hebrew words of Scripture into the more universal language of numbers.

During afternoon study hours, Mila whispered to

Atara, 'Did you notice? The letters in the word מָשִׁיחַ (*messiah*) sum to 358, which equals the sum of נָחָשׁ (*snake*).' Mila recounted the commentary: This equation corroborated that redemption and sin were not exclusive of each other. *Fear not to go down to Egypt*, the Lord tells Jacob; Jacob must go *down* before he can raise a great nation. Descent for the sake of ascent. Redemption *through* sin was a sign of messianic times.

Most of all, Mila cherished the third Sabbath meal at the seminary, when all the girls sang and danced and circled Queen Sabbath to detain her a bit longer. In the last glimmer of sundown, the girls intoned longingly, *Prophet Elijah, come to us with the messiah*, and Mila day-dreamed: Who among them would give birth to the messiah, son of David, who among the girls would deliver the world from suffering?

AFTER ALL THE YEARS during which Atara's secular reading had pulled them apart, Mila loved to prepare for classes with Atara, she loved how Atara studied every page of the Mikraoth Gedoloth, the Expanded Rabbinic Bible, not just the assigned commentaries. Teachers began to call on Atara to explain obscure passages, and classmates consulted her during study hours.

Yet, however earnestly Atara tried to embrace the seminary, Mila feared that it might not last. She could tell from the rigidity with which Atara listened to the rabbis' lectures that they did not satisfy her.

One morning, a teacher called on Atara to sum up a rabbinic argument and Atara wondered aloud about the merit of the argument. The teacher rubbed his eyelids. Mila bit her lip. The class fell still. 'Next verse,' the teacher called.

Another day, Atara raised her hand and asked how Rashi had arrived at an interpretation. 'Such a shame you're not a boy!' the rabbi exclaimed. The class understood it was a shame because boys, not girls, needed good heads to study Torah. Then the rabbi quoted another Rashi passage that gave the same reading and he moved on to the next commentator.

'He repeated the interpretation but didn't explain it,' Atara whispered in Mila's ear.

The rabbi noticed Atara's frown and whisper. 'Is it possible you have something to add to Rashi?' the rabbi asked.

The class laughed.

But then Sabbath came again, the singing, the dancing. Girls at the seminary who knew of Zalman's voice asked Atara to sing. After hearing her once, the girls asked Atara to sing every Friday night. The first measures trembled but soon the notes freed themselves. Some girls closed their eyes. When Atara finished singing, girls lined up to shake her hand. 'May your strength be firm!' Mila, who recognised Zalman's modulations in Atara's song, felt certain that Atara would find her place as the daughter of Zalman and all the generations past.

★

MILA AND ATARA were studying in the little library under the eave when the door crept open. A grey triangular goatee floated between door and jamb. The goatee retreated. The girls stifled a laugh. 'I wonder why he does that,' Atara whispered, returning to the Expanded Rabbinic Bible, but Mila could no longer focus, she was aware of the deep silence around them, that once again Atara and she were the last ones in the Lecture House after study hours, when all the other girls were in their rooms preparing themselves for lights-out.

'ATARA? . . .' The rabbi's voice no longer held warm expectation when he called on her in class.

The words she was finding to formulate her question frightened Atara. The question might begin: When the Bible commands to kill babies and animals, in warfare – or, When God commands that a child suffer for his parents' sin . . . To Atara, these seemed good questions, with implications in *real* life, questions that might matter to Mila, too, but Atara's pulse quickened when the rabbi's dark eyes came to rest on her raised hand, her throat contracted; her voice would quake and strangle as it did every time she tried to ask this kind of question.

'Nothing – I'm sorry.'

One hand came down as the other scribbled *Nuremberg*. Reading about the Nuremberg defence, Atara had understood with out translation, the words were the same in Yiddish: Befehl ist Befehl, *an order is an order*; they were following orders, the Nazis had said. To Atara, it seemed a good question, whether one should ever obey orders blindly, but Rabbi Braunsdorfer might rail: 'Are you,

God forbid, equating the Lord's command to a Hitler command?'

Atara's pen hatched diagonal lines over *Nuremberg*, hatched, cross-hatched, stippled — short lines of equal weight, dots of equal circumference, her pen stamped another pattern of closure, to honour the Lord. The dots filled the margin, the margin bled onto the page—

'Miss Star, would you translate sternly ...' Rabbi Braunsdorfer liked to pun on all the girls' names and *Atara Stern*, which combined *crown* and *star*, stimulated the inclination.

Atara read the Hebrew text and translated: *'Measure for measure the Lord punishes, the Lord is just ...'*

'Thank you. The holy Chazon Isch, peace be upon his soul, explains: Before the war, Jewish parents sent their children to secular schools; they kept their children's bodies alive while sacrificing their souls. *Measure for measure* the Lord struck these parents; He destroyed their children's bodies.' Rabbi Braunsdorfer's voice rose to a high nasal pitch. 'And it was an act of grace! In an act of grace, HaShem relieved these Polish communities of free will before they deteriorated entirely.

'Some murdered children belonged to God-fearing parents? Then suffering must be attributed to Bitul Torah: not enough Torah. And when there was enough Torah, the suffering of innocents must be attributed to yesurim shel ahava, the torments of love; God torments the few who do not sin to permit them to reach a higher station in the next world.'

Atara had stopped taking notes. She did not wait for Rabbi Braunsdorfer to call on her.

'Does the Lord stay to watch, when children are burning?'

Heads turned.

Rabbi Braunsdorfer pulled back his chair.

The bell rang.

Rabbi Braunsdorfer closed his Expanded Rabbinic Bible and descended from the platform. There was a pause, and the usual roar of the girls' pent-up voices exploded in the classroom. Atara's pulse quieted down.

Nothing had happened. She had asked a real question and nothing had happened.

She was leaving the little library under the eave when she came nose-to-nose with the principal regaining his balance as if his ear had been glued to the door. They stood on the landing; she in her plaid dress, her lace collar; he in his grey suit and grey goatee – he was short for a man. He did not look straight into her eyes but to a point behind her right shoulder. His goatee lifted as he swallowed.

'Dirty hands take hold of sacred texts vizout approofed mediashun.'

'Pardon?'

He enunciated slowly. 'Dirty hands take hold of sacred texts vizout approofed mediation.'

Dirty hands? She had been studying holy books, not forbidden books.

'Should I not use the library?'

His right hand moved in circles as he spoke. 'Some zink: I do not have to study zis but out of choice I vill. Neverzeless, it is not petter. To study vat you are not commanded to study is mental exercise – like crossvord puzzle or chess, but here, in zis school, ve do not seek to stimulate ze mind.'

'No?'

'In zis school, ve seek to stimulate ze soul – ze *soul*, not ze mind. If a girl vants to uplift her soul and be near ze Creator, she studies vat she is *commanded* to study. Do you know ze rules of tennis doubles? In doubles, you stick to your side of ze court. Only a busybody rushes onto her partner's side. Poaching never pays: you leaf your side of ze court open and you spoil ze game. Ven you open a holy pook, ask: Am I entering someone else's territory? Zink about it. Good night.'

The principal started down the stairs. Atara saw him in tennis whites, running after the ball on his side of the court . . .

Despite the principal's warning, Atara returned to the low-ceilinged library. Now, when she opened a book, the letters scolded: 'Tsk tsk . . . *dirty hands*! Moses received the Law at Sinai and passed it on to Joshua, who passed it on to the Elders, who passed it on to the Prophets, who passed it on to the Men of the Great Assembly; they did not pass it on to Atara, daughter of Hannah.'

★

THE PRINCIPAL called Mila into his office before Passover break.

'Zo, you are returning to Paris ... Are you curious about ze world, outside?'

Mila protested. Everyone was curious, sometimes, but her deepest desire was to marry a son of Torah and raise a Jewish family.

'Good, good. Zen you must not befriend evildoers.'

Mila nodded.

'You vant to help Atara, yes?'

Mila's heart beat faster.

'Vat does Atara vant? Vat are her zoughts, her plans?'

The words Atara might have used almost left Mila's mouth, *Atara wants to make her own choices,* but instead Mila offered: 'Atara studies more intensely than any girl here.'

The principal cleared his throat. 'Is Atara interested in boys?'

'Of course not!'

'Zen vy, vy does she not accept answers zat are clear? You and all her friends must show Atara you disapprove.' His finger wagged. 'It is an obligation to hate ze vicked. Show her zat she vill lose you.' He paused. 'You, too, are in danger. Reputation iz a fragile vase, one false move ze vase breaks ... vat, vat else do you have, poor orphan?' His thick lenses muddled the colour of his eyes. 'Zink about it.' He rose. 'Have a safe trip and kosher Passover.'

Mila stumbled out. Atara's questions were getting

them both in trouble. One girl had even asked whether Atara came from a freier (*free-thinking*) home and why had she been admitted to the seminary? The habitually agreeable Mila had snapped: 'Atara's father is the great Torah scholar Zalman Stern who follows the Rebbe's every edict.'

★

MILA AND ATARA kissed Zalman's hand, they kissed and hugged Hannah as the younger children tugged at their sleeves and skirts; they kissed and hugged their siblings. Atara noticed Schlomo, just thirteen and returned the day before from his yeshiva abroad. Schlomo stood at a distance, biting his lower lip – a bar mitzvah boy does not kiss a sister even after a lengthy separation. Atara waved to him, awkwardly; the boy flushed and stormed away.

Hannah pressed a hand against her lower back and let out a short moan. Atara rushed with a chair. 'Sit, Mama, sit!'

Mila rushed with a low stool. 'Here, Auntie Hannah, here!'

Hannah sat and sighed with relief. 'My daughters are home.'

Atara lifted Hannah's swollen foot, placed it on the stool; Mila lifted the other swollen foot, placed it on the stool. Hannah smiled, extended her legs. The light bounced off the tight mesh of her compression stockings as off a metal plate.

The backs of Hannah's knees were knotted plums, her feet were purple deltas. The doctor had warned and threatened, but what were high blood pressure, varicose veins and exhaustion when one considered Hannah's siblings who never returned? Hannah's belly had swelled again.

Leaning back in the chair, Hannah said, 'Now tell me, my Torah scholar girls, what have you learned? Tell me everything.'

Mila turned to Atara. 'Now, when we open a T'nach, we read not only Rashi but also Sforno and Ibn Ezra and—'

Hannah leapt up to grab the coin a toddler was pushing up his nose.

Atara had leapt faster. 'Sit, Mama, sit!'

Every day, Mila and Atara schemed and strategised so Hannah would rest her rounding belly. They took over Passover cleaning. From early morning until late at night, they hunted crumbs of unleavened bread. They sang as they scoured the seams of the parquet and behind bookshelves and armoires; they sang the French songs that made Atara melancholy for the lycée and the new seminary songs that Mila liked best. At times, Mila scampered up to Atara and kissed her cheek — best friends, sisters for life. Atara kissed her back, for life.

A couple of times, Mila fell out of harmony. Atara held the note, waiting for Mila to find her voice again, but Mila ran out of the room.

Vat, vat else do you have, poor orphan?

At the seminary, where no other girl had parents nearby, Mila had felt less of an orphan, but the principal had chosen to remind her.

Mila leaned over the baby's crib, pressed her cheek against the soft baby skin. Every thing was limpid when she looked into his wide eyes, when she tickled him under the chin and he gurgled with rapture.

'Milenka, the baby needs sleep,' Hannah called.

Mila stepped away from the crib.

If the Lord asked for the baby? Mila tiptoed back to the crib. The baby cooed, wiggled arms and legs. Mila hugged her elbows and rocked from side to side; she leaned into the crib, kissed the baby's cheeks, wildly, kissed his tiny toes. The Lord would not ask for *this* baby.

During the middle days of Passover, the girls coaxed Hannah into accompanying the children to the Luxembourg Gardens. When Hannah sat on a park bench and turned her wan face to the sun, when Hannah inhaled deeply, as magnolia petals settled pink and white on the spring lawn, the girls were euphoric – Hannah was tasting life, this life. But the lull soon faded. Someone somewhere needed Mama's attention, prodding, protruding duties, more urgent than an ache for rest. The girls crashed from paradise, to Hannah's abrupt hurry. Hannah gripped a toddler's hand and heaved her heavy belly far from magnolia alley, while other mothers sat on the park benches.

THE RETURN to the seminary neared and Mila grew unsure of herself, of what things meant; she changed her mind and changed it again. What did the principal want her to do? Was Atara in danger?

.   .   .

First Schlomo left for his yeshiva abroad, then the girls prepared to leave.

Hannah called them into the living room; she opened the dark walnut chest and showed them the fine eiderdowns and white nightgowns, prettier than any nightgown Mila or Atara had ever worn. 'The Lord willing, the chest will soon be full.' Hannah kissed her girls, enjoined them to heed their reputations. The entire family stood on the balcony as the taxi turned the corner. *May the Lord bless you. May He guard your steps* ...

★

THE HOUSING assignments had been changed. Mila now shared a room with the most popular girls at the seminary, including two cousins from a wealthy family who had spent the war years in Switzerland.

Atara shared a room with girls who devoted the longest time to prayers; quiet girls who blushed when it was their turn to read aloud a verse; girls who would never raise a hand to ask a question.

'Mila, here!' In the front row of the classroom, Zissi and Goldie, the two cousins from Switzerland, waved and pointed to the empty seat between them.

Mila did not notice Atara entering the classroom, did not notice Atara's surprise when she saw that Mila had not kept a seat for her. Now Atara and Mila would sit apart in class all semester. It was deemed unfriendly to ask to switch seats.

When the lunch bell sounded, Mila's neighbours whisked her to the dining hall where they steered her to their table, bubbling their admiration for Rabbi Braunsdorfer's intellect and wit; the girls were agreed, Rabbi Braunsdorfer's classes in Jewish Thought were the most uplifting.

Mila noticed there was no seat for Atara at her table. When Atara entered the hall, Mila's chest tightened. It would be hard to switch tables later.

Atara found a seat in the rear.

When Mila looked back, Atara was shredding a slice of bread, crushing the crumbs between her fingers, rolling the crumbs into pellets. Mila pushed back her chair and rose.

'But Mila, you must say grace at the same table where you blessed the bread!'

Mila's hands gripped the edge of the table. It was important to make new friends. It was immature to do everything with Atara. She let herself fall back into her chair.

Zissi resumed her story: 'We were telling you about our Passover excursion on the Lac Leman . . .'

Mila turned her head. A T3 girl was whispering in Atara's ear. Atara stopped rolling pellets of dough and brushed the crumbs aside; it was forbidden to waste bread.

On the Sabbath, Atara went to fetch Mila for their weekly walk, but Mila had been invited to the home of a rabbi teacher, to take care of the babies. Mila's room-mates reminded Atara that it was a good deed to take care of a teacher's babies, and it was also practice.

Mila returned just in time for the Third Meal.

When the girls rose to circle the holiness of the Sabbath, Zissi and Goldie held Mila's hands as Mila's gaze searched for Atara. When Mila saw Atara standing near the door, Mila's eyes pleaded, inviting Atara into the round, but the circle spun faster, every three steps, the circle hopped, Mila between Zissi and Goldie.

Atara noticed Zissi's headband in Mila's hair.

She could still hear the girls' singing as she climbed the stairs to the little library. She opened an Expanded Rabbinic Bible. As dusk filled the room, the letters blurred and lifted from the page, they turned, hopped, and circled. Her hand pressed onto the open book. The letters fell back into place, Scripture centre top, gloss both sides and below.

She started to read, but again the letters stirred, the lines written centuries apart joined and then marched together, circling her future in a changeless round of faith – nothing new could happen, not since Moses at Sinai.

But then one letter escaped and spiralled out of the room. Soon more letters hovered and spun in their own directions. She pressed her hands on the open book but the letters kept lifting, hopping, unfurling into open shapes that turned, turned ... turned into the lycée's forbidden poems and maths formulae. Laboratories, experiments, alembics, stylish bell skirts swayed on the horizon in dazzling galaxies ... Ah, to think gratuitous human constructs!

Would Zalman ever permit college? Would he permit the *baccalauréat*? Or even the lycée? If she told him how hard she had tried at the seminary?

Then, after the *baccalauréat*, she would propose to study ... not painting, too frivolous; not literature either, where people made choices. Certainly not philosophy. Medicine? If she asked to study medicine ... a life modelled on Albert Schweitzer's, in Africa, such a life would be worthwhile and when she was not in Africa helping to save people, it would not be sinful to make a living ...

She would speak to Zalman during summer break, she must.

In June, news that the government of Israel might collapse spread through the classrooms. There were no newspapers, no radios, no televisions in the seminary. The girls debated whether the implosion of the blasphemous Zionist leadership meant that the Lord might soon forgive the sins of the People of Israel, whether the messiah was coming, the dead resurrecting. That Sabbath, the girls danced with special fervour. They asked that Atara lead an *I believe*. Atara hummed the melody and the hall filled with the girls' longing voices: *I believe with entire faith in the coming of the messiah...*

Summer 1956

BACK IN PARIS FOR SUMMER BREAK, THE GIRLS
divided the chores. Atara took responsibility for Zalman's
study. Every morning, she dusted the shelves of
Babylonian and Jerusalem Talmud, the holy books that
had come with the family from Transylvania, and the
holy books Zalman ordered from Jewish presses all over
the world. She would find the right time to speak to
her father. She dusted the curved back of the walnut
armchair, the studded leather armrests, the claw feet,
and day-dreamed about a day of classes at the Sorbonne,
followed by dinner at home with her parents and siblings.
She breathed in the faint, gamey smell of the piebald
cowhide that held Zalman's prayer shawl and phylacteries. She straightened the pile of *Der Yid*, the weekly
from America that disseminated the Rebbe's speeches
and edicts.

The editorial page raged against Zionist leaders who
failed to warn Hungarian communities about deportations, against Zionist leaders who selected fellow
Zionists for rescue and crossed off millions of God-fearers
whom they did not deem fit for their state. It was
forbidden to participate in the Zionist abomination; it

was forbidden to enlist in the Zionist army; it was forbidden to vote – the Rebbe of Satmar was offering fifteen dollars' worth of foodstuff to anyone agreeing not to participate in the Zionist elections – were six million not enough?

In August, Atara was still looking for the right moment to speak to her father. Every day she stood outside Zalman's study and listened as he practised for the High Holy Days service, his singing voice so full of grace and balance . . . One afternoon, when everything was quiet on the other side of the door, she gathered her courage and knocked.

'Nu?' Zalman called, his clear blue eyes lifting from a Talmud tome as she opened the door.

'Tatta?'

'Nu?'

'I studied hard . . . I tried . . .' Her voice shook. 'Tatta, would you permit that I not return to the seminary?'

Zalman's lips widened into a smile. 'Certainly you can stay home. I am still suspicious of these new schools for girls. Countless generations of Jewish mothers raised Torah scholars without knowing even how to read Scripture. And your help around the house would be a blessing. Of course you can stay home.'

'I'll help around the house and with the children.'

'Nu?' Zalman still smiled.

'Would you permit – would it be acceptable – at night, when all the work is done . . . would it be acceptable if I studied? With books. From my room. I would not come in contact with anyone.'

'What kind of books?'

'I was thinking . . . hoping – after I marry of course, I was hoping to study medicine to help—'

'Medicine?' Zalman repeated, unbelieving. 'You think there were not enough Jewish *doctors* in Germany? You *know* it is forbidden to follow a curriculum of secular studies.'

'I was hoping to help save lives . . . to—'

Zalman tried to calm himself. 'You are almost a grown woman and soon it will be up to your husband, but until then, it is my obligation to protect you, even against your will. I must make sure you do not blemish the name of our family and jeopardise your future and your siblings' future.'

'Tatta, I have tried. I have not read the wrong books for more than a year.'

'You have come under bad influences and you will come to your senses, you must, or I will lock you up in this apartment until I walk you to the wedding dais. And hear me well: If you do not follow our fathers' way, you will fail at whatever you undertake. You will sink from one depravity to the next. You will wander the world and never find a home.'

THE LAST summer afternoons in the Luxembourg Gardens, while Mila watched the children in the playground, Atara rose and circled the water basin, the ringing alleys, the park fence. She synched her steps to those of strangers so that they would take her to different fates. The postman on his bicycle, she envied him, envied his wheels kissing the cobbles, that he knew one language only, one country only, envied his undivided past, undivided from his future.

T2

'*IF* YOU WERE AMONG THE GREAT ONES IN ISRAEL, you might be permitted to inquire into Creation. But *us? Us?*' Droplets of spit shot out of Rabbi Braunsdorfer's mouth, hung above the lectern, and settled on the first row. 'Asked improper questions, the believer answers: I *refuse*! Asked about so-called contradictions in Genesis, the believer shows respect for the Lord and replies: I *refuuuse* – I refuse to think about it!' Bang, the fist landed on the lectern. Pause. 'In our sweet Torahleh,' the voice dropped to a whisper, 'the Lord gives us all that we need to know.'

From Atara's seat in the back row, the classes melded one into the other. The rabbi's finger-wagging about 'things not for us to ask' seemed remote.

The previous year, Atara had looked forward to the classes in history, but at the seminary, the classes in history, too, were classes in faith. It was lack of faith that brought pogroms and destructions, and the person who failed to connect Jewish tragedies to sin caused further suffering.

When she leaned sideways, Atara could see Mila in the front row, back erect when Mila followed the lecture, back slumped or chin lifted when she day-dreamed. Mila found comfort in this ordered world where sin explained suffering. Sometimes Mila's head turned back, her long lashes coming down just before her gaze met Atara's. Mila's head inclined as she took assiduous notes, her nape shaded by tendrils escaping her new beehive hairdo, modelled after Zissi's.

Atara started to skip afternoon study hours. She sneaked away after lunch, when the girls surged out of the dining hall. She ran past the Bewick and Eyre crossing, which was as far as she had ever gone on her Sabbath walks with Mila.

Up the hill, a tall shaft sputtered an orange flame. She turned back.

The door of a bar opened. A bent silhouette stumbled out, cupped cigarette to mouth, and teetered in front of a car bumper. Cracked singing spilled onto the kerb, about a canary going silent in a mine. In another life, she might have known what the canary song was about, she might have spoken to these people; in her life, she could not be seen talking to a non-Jew. She walked on. The street ended in front of a slag heap. She turned back.

A barge moaned downriver. On the tar-dark riverbank, blue-clad workers leaned over fires in tin drums, small hells in the early night.

On High Street, a car veered and spattered her coat.

She heard the girls as soon as she turned onto the seminary's block, heard the stamping feet — did passers-by wonder what kind of life warranted so much singing and dancing? Time and again, the dining tables were pushed against the walls, the chairs piled high against the tables, and Atara sighed with relief; no one would have noticed her absence in the excitement that followed the news of a girl's engagement. In the cleared space, the girls were wound in circles, some facing into the centre, some facing out. Zissi, Mila, Goldie danced arm over arm.

Atara's study partner caught sight of Atara and broke away from the round. 'I looked for you, Bless the Lord you are here . . .'

The girls' speech pattern also grated on Atara's nerves, the ready-made locutions.

'Atara is here!' a voice called.

'Is she singing, is Atara singing?'

'Not now,' Atara whispered to no one in particular.

'Atara will sing!'

Atara stepped back.

A T3 girl who stood by the door rebuked Atara: 'It is a mitzvah to be happy on such a joyous occasion.'

Atara wanted to quiet the singing; she wanted to speak up, loud, so that all the girls would hear; she wanted to share with them that in the library in Paris, she had read that the Nazis could have been defeated much earlier if forces had united, but religious leaders, fearing assimilation, chose to organise *against* the Bolsheviks who were fighting the Nazis, chose not to unite with less religious or secular Jews. Atara's mouth opened but what came out was a sound like the bleating of a sheep. Her hands came to her ears, to block the echoing bleats. She stumbled out.

Every morning, she woke to the same impasse. Could she marry a Hasid who expected a Hasidic wife to cherish orthodox life? Would she raise children, who, in turn, would be forbidden to read secular books?

Climbing the stairs to the classroom, her calves

cramped. Sitting in front of the Expanded Rabbinic Bible, her scalp itched.

Was it not better to *choose* one's death and die all at once?

March 1957

MILA AND ATARA HAD BEEN AT THE SEMINARY A
year and a half when the principal called Atara into his
office. Zalman had written a letter, Hannah was having a
difficult pregnancy and the doctor prescribed bed rest.
Zalman asked that one of the girls come home. The principal thought Atara should go. Let Mila benefit a bit
longer from the seminary's teachings since her T2 year
might be cut short . . . there had been enquiries . . .

'Mila is getting engaged?'

'Shh . . . enquiries only. You mustn't disturb Mila's
peace of mind.'

Atara was packing when Mila came running.

'Auntie Hannah isn't well? I'm going with you. I am!'

The girls boarded the train to London, they scanned
the rows of tired upholstered seats, wiggled their heavy
suitcases into an empty row, sat in the row behind.

'You think Auntie Hannah is very sick?' Mila asked.

'No, it must be as my father wrote, she's having a difficult pregnancy and he needs help with the children and
cooking. If it were serious, he would have asked that we
both come home. Don't be afraid, Mila.'

'Then why are you so upset?'

'I'm not . . . I . . . Mila, do you feel ready to marry?'

Mila lifted a shoulder and let it drop; she smiled; she brushed her new short fringe to the side.

'*I* don't feel ready at all,' Atara said.

The girls stared at the unfolding landscape, the terraced houses, mining shafts, once again painfully aware of the distance between them. *Deaf Hill, Stony Heap* . . . What had happened? *Newton Aycliffe, Doncaster* . . . They kept silent.

They alighted in London and transferred from King's Cross station to Charing Cross station, where they waited for the train to Dover. In the crowded waiting area, newspapers crackled as pages turned and folded.

A headline caught Atara's attention:

ZIONIST OFFICIAL SHOT
Collaborated with Eichmann

Atara was familiar with the Rebbe's fulminations against Zionists, but this was a secular paper. She nudged Mila. 'Look!'

Mila shrugged a shoulder. 'What do you expect? Zionists have no morals.'

Atara stepped up to the news kiosk. She stared at the black-and-white photograph under *Collaborated with Eichmann*: boxcars with open doors, people climbing up, down, standing nearby; some in Hasidic garb.

She searched her purse for coins. She looked right and left to make sure no one from her father's world or from the seminary's world was there to see her.

'You're buying a Goyish paper?' Mila asked, alarmed.

Dragging her heavy suitcase, Mila marched towards

the train pulling into the station. 'I'm not sitting next to you if you're going to read that,' Mila said when Atara caught up with her.

Atara dragged her suitcase down the narrow centre aisle of the carriage, she thanked the man who helped her lift her suitcase onto the luggage rack, took a seat. Once more, she examined the photograph.

The Kasztner Train, Budapest, June 30, 1944, the caption said.

She started to read. An agent of the Zionist Rescue Mission in Hungary, Rezsö Kasztner, had been accused of collaboration. A long trial in Israel surfaced conflicting accounts. Kasztner considered himself a hero for having the audacity to negotiate with Eichmann in Nazi-occupied Budapest and saving as many as he could, but the court concluded that Kasztner obtained safe passage for a few by agreeing to keep the rest from resisting deportation.

Witnesses who had lost their families in Auschwitz testified that Kasztner's people circulated fake postcards from Kenyérmezö – the Hungarian breadbasket: *We are resettling. There is food, work* . . . Those who heard about the cards thought: Why flee and endanger anyone's life? They boarded the cattle cars.

Others testified that Kasztner sent Halutzim, Zionist pioneers, to warn Hungarian communities, but the people would not listen. One woman recalled that in the town of Szatmár, the rabbi, Joel Teitelbaum, threatened to excommunicate the Zionist youth who tried to warn his congregation.

Atara paused. It felt odd to see the name of the Rebbe in a secular paper, a national daily. She stared again at the photograph and suddenly realised where she had seen the image before: in the countless tellings of Mila's dream.

Open boxcars with Jews in them.

Atara sprang up, eager to confirm Mila's version of her mother's death: There had been a train of open boxcars in Hungary, in the spring of '44. She stopped – the caption under the photograph mentioned Budapest, but Mila's parents were fleeing deportations from Kolozvár. And the Rebbe lived in Szatmár. She needed more information before she awakened Mila's memories, she needed to be sure, she needed the train's itinerary and the date it departed, she needed a list of passengers . . .

In Dover, she caught headlines on a newsstand:

KASZTNER IN CRITICAL CONDITION

THE KASZTNER AFFAIR

She rushed down and bought two more papers. Once again, she saw mention of the Satmarer Rebbe. The *prominenten,* the people Kasztner had saved, had not come forward to testify in his favour during the eighteen-month trial; they had not wanted to be identified as owing their lives to him.

Kasztner asked for testimony of the grand rabbi Joel Teitelbaum, the Rebbe of the Satmar Hasidim, but the latter refused.

'Kasztner did not save me, God did,' said the Rebbe of Satmar.

The Rebbe of Satmar was on Kasztner's train! Again, Atara wanted to run to Mila, but Mila would get angry if Atara suggested the Rebbe was linked to a Zionist venture. She needed more information. She read on.

The paper retold the judge's verdict: Kasztner *sold his soul to the devil* when he sacrificed the mass of Hungarian Jews for a chosen few.

One editorial noted that Kasztner's negotiations mirrored the stance of many Jewish leaders who agreed to the Nazi distinction between elite Jews and the masses — an agreement especially problematic in Hungary, where Jewish leaders knew where the cattle cars were headed; in April '44, two escapees from Auschwitz, Rudolf Vrba and Alfred Wetzler, had informed Hungarian leaders, in detail, about the crematoria.

Atara stopped reading. Had the Rebbe of Szatmár been informed? Had he warned his community before fleeing? She scanned the tight print for *Joel Teitelbaum, Szatmár, Satmar, Satmarer Rebbe* . . .

A first contingent, 388 elect Jews out of 18,000 in the ghetto of Cluj (Kolozvár), in Transylvania . . .

Kolozvár, Mila's hometown.

If the Rebbe was part of the Kolozvár contingent, then Mila's mother could have seen him.

Boarding the ferry to Calais, Atara spent her last coins on a magazine.

The contingent from Cluj arrived in Budapest on June 10, 1944, and was placed in a guarded, privileged camp in the courtyard of the Wechselmann Institute for the Deaf, on Columbus Street.

June 10, 1944, was a Sabbath day. The Rebbe of the Satmar Hasidim, Joel Teitelbaum, would not carry his prayer shawl and phylacteries from the railway station to Columbus Street . . .

The Rebbe was on the contingent that left Kolozvár.

Atara rose. She wanted to apologise for doubting the story Mila had needed her so much to believe, about Mila's mother running to the Rebbe . . .

On a bench in the ferry's passenger cabin, Mila was reading *Lives of Our Holy Rebbes*. She looked up when Atara called her name, and frowned when she saw the stack of newspapers in Atara's hands. Just then, the loudspeaker sputtered that passengers should gather their belongings and prepare for customs. Out of the large cabin windows, Atara saw the deckhands already mooring the ferry to the dock. She would have to wait until they had gone through customs before speaking to Mila.

Holding their stateless papers instead of passports, the girls walked up to the customs officer. Atara's heart fluttered as it had at previous border crossings, but other thoughts distracted her, thoughts of how much it would mean to Mila, that the circumstances of a special train, the circumstances of her mother's death, could be validated. She also thought of how this new information might affect her relationship with Mila. Perhaps, once Mila learned that the Rebbe owed his life to a Zionist venture, to the very Zionist who negotiated with Eichmann, Mila might understand some of Atara's doubts, might begin to question the Rebbe's infallibility.

On the journey from Calais to Paris, in the intimacy of a compartment they had to themselves, Atara sat next to Mila and took her hand. She showed Mila the photograph of the open boxcars. She apologised for not believing Mila's version of her mother's death.

Mila stared at the photograph.

'It was a special train,' Atara explained, 'that's why the doors were open. It was a train of *prominenten* and the

Rebbe was on it and the first contingent left from Kolozvár—'

'Kolozvár?' Mila's voice trembled when she uttered the name of her hometown. 'But the Rebbe lived in Szatmár, not Kolozvár.'

Atara told Mila what she had read about the Rebbe's escape: the Rebbe had fled Szatmár in secret, in the middle of the night, but was caught before reaching Romania and was placed in the Kolozvár ghetto, where he heard of the Zionist train for *prominenten.*

'The Rebbe would never deal with a Zionist,' Mila said flatly. 'And the Rebbe was deported.'

'He was *not* deported.'

'To Bergen-Belsen.'

'Have you heard of regular Jewish deportees travelling from Bergen-Belsen to Switzerland *during* the war? The Rebbe spent five months in Bergen-Belsen because Kasztner's negotiations were complicated, but all the people on Kasztner's train were *Exchange Jews.* It meant that they had enough food. They didn't work. Families weren't separated. Even newborn babies survived, and old people, too. The Rebbe was not deported.'

'To Bergen-Belsen . . .' Mila said barely audibly. Then: 'And this special train stopped where my parents were hiding?'

'I don't know why it stopped but it's as you always said: You saw the Rebbe.'

'What if I didn't? What if I thought I recognised him but it wasn't him?'

'Your mother saw him. You said she yelled "Rebbe!" when she ran out.'

Mila sank under the weight of the tragedy returning to her. Her eyes closed. As if articulating an unspeakable doubt, she whispered, 'But if the Rebbe could stop the train in front of our hiding place, why couldn't he save us?'

Atara did not have the heart to tell Mila that when the Rebbe boarded Kasztner's train, he had already decided to leave her family behind. 'You said the other trains, too, slowed around the bend. It wasn't the Rebbe who stopped the train.'

'But when my mother ran out, was she trying to save him or was she hoping he would save us?'

'She must have hoped – your parents must have known about the Kasztner train, everyone in the ghetto knew, everyone tried—' Atara stopped. She feared that if Mila learned from her the specifics of the Rebbe's escape, then Mila might dismiss the information as more of Atara's questioning. She thought she must create a direct encounter between Mila and this new information. She held back the facts and feelings rushing through her, and rolled them all into one bold request: 'Mila, there are maps, train schedules. There are witness accounts. We can find out every detail about Kasztner's train and about the Rebbe's escape. We can find out the exact date the train left Kolozvár and map its itinerary, we can find out what the people on Kasztner's train knew about where the rest of the community was going. Mila, will you come with me to the library?'

'The *library*?'

'To find out what happened, what happened in *your* life.'

Mila was silent, but she did not refuse.

The night of their arrival in Paris, the idea that they might go together to the library hovered between the girls. Atara, emboldened, took out the transistor radio she kept hidden on the armoire's top shelf, a tiny radio she had traded with a former classmate during her last year at the lycée. Ears glued to the crackling speaker, hair interwoven on the same pillow, the girls listened for news of Kasztner and the Kasztner affair. Kasztner's condition had worsened. The girls thought of the dying man. Had a Jew really collaborated with Nazis? Had the Rebbe boarded a special train negotiated by a Zionist? To the girls, the two questions seemed equally inconceivable.

They did not turn off the radio after the news. French songs followed one after the other and soon the girls floated on rhythms where non-Jew and Jew throbbed to the same longings, boy and girl walking hand in hand and never letting go . . .

The next day, when they woke, Atara reminded Mila of the research they needed to do. Mila nodded solemnly. In the morning the two girls cleaned the apartment. After lunch, Hannah encouraged them to go to the Luxembourg Gardens for a last carefree walk before the children – who had been distributed among orthodox families when Hannah was assigned to bed rest – came home.

Atara mentioned the library as soon as the two girls were outside. Again, Mila nodded, but when they reached the rue Soufflot that led to the Bibliothèque Sainte-Geneviève, Mila threaded her arm in Atara's elbow and steered her towards the Luxembourg.

For the first time in years, the girls entered the gardens without pram or tow of siblings. They felt giddy, and slightly guilty, strolling down the chestnut-lined alley, just the two of them. The end of winter was in the air. They leaned against the balustrade overlooking the pond. Pigeons basked in the warmer rays, feathers puffed around their tiny heads. The Sénat clock struck the hour and the girls wished that it would always be so, the two of them, together, watching the seasons change.

After the last chime had faded, Atara said, 'There's no one in Paris, no one in all of France whose pedigree is good enough for Zalman Stern. We'll be married far from Paris—'

'No one will marry us off without our consent.'

'But our *only* choice is to consent. Mila . . . if I were courageous enough . . . if I prepared the baccalauréat and went to college, would you—'

'Courageous to go to college? What's courageous is to remain a Jew.'

'But if I did go to college and my father disowned me, would I lose you, too?'

Mila stepped towards the large planters that gardeners in blue shifts were wheeling out of the orangerie. She read out the labels: *'Palmier-dattier, Laurier-rose, Grenadier*—' She turned to Atara. 'When my parents live again, I want them to recognise me as a Jew. I want them to recognise my children. I want them to recognise *your* children.'

'And if your parents don't — if the messiah doesn't come in your lifetime?'

'Aneini! *Answer me!*' Mila called to the sky and her arms flew up as she spun on her tiptoes in front of a parterre of tulips; blue, white, red tulips, the colours of France casting long shadows on the freshly seeded lawn. 'The messiah will come and we'll fly to Jerusalem . . .'

Nurserymen pushing wheelbarrows of potted plants turned their heads and whistled. Mila's hem covered her knees, her long-sleeved blouse was buttoned to the neck, but she looked graceful spinning with her narrow waist and her tall up-do. Mila and Atara hooked elbows. They skipped under the chestnut trees, out of the Luxembourg; they skipped above the paving seams of the rue Servandoni, across the boulevard Saint-Germain, along the rue de Seine. On the crest of the Pont des Arts, they leaned over the bridge's railing and turned up their palms for the first drops of rain. The sky unleashed itself and they whirled as they had as children, arms stretched wide as their tongues searched their lips for the taste of clouds. Streetlamps were twinkling stars ... Atara flew above river and roofs, above all the boundaries the world drew around her. Mila whirled faster still, until she let herself drop to the ground, too dizzy to answer Atara's calls. When Mila's eyes opened, they were filled, not with Atara's inebriation but with apology – for surviving, for being alive. Atara combed her fingers through Mila's dishevelled hair, combed them towards what she hoped might still be the direction of an escape.

On the quai de la Mégisserie, shop owners carried twittering birdcages indoors; roller shutters rattled shut. It was late. They would go to the library tomorrow. The girls started to run.

They arrived home, cheeks flushed as in childhood. Tiptoeing into the entry, they found Hannah and Zalman sitting in the living room, waiting for them, but rather than question where the girls had been and why they looked so exhilarated, Hannah and Zalman smiled, warmly taking them in.

'Go, quick, dry yourselves or you'll catch cold,' Hannah said. 'Come back when you're done.' Again, she smiled. 'We have something to tell you.'

When the girls returned with towels wrapped around their hair, Zalman spoke first. 'We are far from the

Rebbe's court, but your lineage, Blimela, and the good reputation of our home make you a commendable match. The phone has been ringing, calls from America . . .'

Hannah's smile widened. 'Word of your beauty seems to have spread as well. We keep saying that you are young, but we received a call to day that had the two of us talking all afternoon.'

'A Torah scholar, a favourite at the Rebbe's court.'

'Handsome, we hear.'

'Surely you remember Josef Lichtenstein?'

Mila caught her breath.

'For years, our Josef was too deep in study to consider any match,' Zalman continued, 'but someone mentioned you, that you were coming of age . . . It appears Josef now has time enough.' Zalman hesitated a moment and then said, 'Josef Lichtenstein spent seven years on a non-Jewish farm, he called a non-Jew *mother*.' Zalman breathed in deeply. 'Blimela, I speak to you as to a daughter: If this young man's upbringing – for which he bears no responsibility, if you have the slightest misgiving about Josef Lichtenstein, you need not agree to meet him, but all the informatzieh is good. His teachers laud him, so do his study partners and every family with whom he spends the Sabbath. Yes, the merit of fathers visits upon their sons, the soul of the holy Rebbe Elimelech Lichtenstein has been watching over our Josef. I must add, Blimela, your parents, may they rest in peace, your parents would have felt honoured to strike a match with the grandnephew of the holy Rebbe Elimelech Lichtenstein.'

That evening, Mila was too restless to lie down. Pacing between the twin brass beds, she talked about Josef, implausible, mystifying Josef – Josef the brave farm boy who was also a Hasidic Jew. Laughingly, then with growing earnestness, her words wove her life and Josef's; marriage with Josef would signify the culmination of their torn and reconstructed childhoods; children with Josef would be the triumph of their parents' world over those who set out to destroy it.

Atara wanted to share Mila's excitement. She remembered liking the boy, and Josef would be different from Zalman, but was it now inevitable that she would lose Mila?

The neighbouring bells of Saint-Paul struck, each gong heavy, solitary. Mila sighed. 'If I no longer heard those bells . . .'

'We've always known that a marriage our parents approved meant giving up Paris and its bells.'

'It isn't a coincidence that I learn of this the day I was so close to going to the library. It's as if Josef were saving me all over again.'

'From the *library*? Josef is saving you from the *library*?'

'I don't need to research it. I know: the Rebbe had to save himself so he could save Judaism.'

'Yes, there must be a holy text, somewhere, that says it's okay to abandon your community if you believe you're saving Judaism,' Atara said with growing hopelessness.

'The Rebbe had to live. Who knows what worse suffering his prayers averted.'

'If the Rebbe boarded that train thinking he was saving Judaism, then he did exactly what so angers him about Zionists selecting young pioneers to salvage *their* vision of Jewry. In the end, Zionists did save their arch-enemy, the Rebbe of Szatmár, whereas he saved himself, his wife—'

'I'm not listening. The Rebbe did what HaShem told him to do.'

'It doesn't bother you that he advised your grandparents to tear up their Palestine Certificates? That he fled with the help of a Zionist?'

They both thought of the Palestine Certificates that Mila's grandparents had obtained before the war and tore up after seeking the Rebbe's advice, a story Zalman had told many times so that Mila would be proud of her lineage, of her grandparents gassed in Auschwitz.

'That was before the war,' Mila said, trembling. 'He gave that advice before the war.'

'Terrible advice. He also expelled from the congregation anyone who had any dealings with Zionists and then, when it was too late for everyone else—'

'Atara, you're really becoming an apikores. I'm not listening.'

'—he saved himself. It didn't occur to him to ask why the Germans might let out this one train of elect Jews? And if it didn't occur to him, should he still decide for us—'

'It was God's will that the Rebbe should live.'

Atara threw her little transistor radio to the floor.

Mila stared, open-mouthed, at the cracked plastic shell, at the knob rolling under the bed.

'And will it be God's will and the Rebbe's will for you to leave *me* behind?' Atara asked.

'The Rebbe is not responsible for what the Nazis did,' Mila whispered.

Tears welled in Atara's eyes. 'Of course the Rebbe is not responsible for what the Nazis did. And neither are the Zionists. The Rebbe behaved like other people who wanted desperately to live, and we can live, too. We don't need to ask the Rebbe or anyone. Mila, if I went to college and my father declared me dead, would you not see me again?'

'You won't. You can't do it to your parents. You can't do

it to me.' Mila started her night prayers after which it was not permitted to speak: *'Michael is to my right, Gabriel to my left…'*

MILA AND JOSEF had not seen each other for ten years. Occasionally visitors from Williamsburg had brought news: the rescued orphan had chanted his bar mitzvah like a true Hasid; the orphan boy lived at the yeshiva in a room with seven other boys and spent Sabbaths with families in Williamsburg. The teller of one story was unsure of whether it was a sign of good or ill, but a menacing dog once strayed into the yeshiva yard and Josef, to the wonderment of all who watched, knew how to appease the unclean animal.

Except for such episodic news, Mila had been left to her fading memories.

Had Josef stayed with the Sterns, had Mila and Josef been raised as brother and sister, had Josef done what other yeshiva boys do – trust that a marriage with a girl he had never met would be arranged for him . . . Instead, Josef waited for the little girl he had rescued when he was a child, for the beautiful Mila Heller who loved Paris but would consider joining the Rebbe's court in Williamsburg, in America.

★

MILA AND JOSEF sat across from each other – she, seventeen, modest but fashionable in her blue taffeta suit and tall up-do; he, twenty-two, face no longer honey-coloured but indoor yeshiva pale under the wide-brimmed black hat.

The door of the dining room was ajar, unmarried men and women must not meet alone.

Unlike the averted eyes of other yeshiva boys, Josef's gaze was direct.

His voice was much deeper than she remembered. *'Mila Heller...'*

'Anghel?...'

He blinked. 'Josef.'

She flushed. 'Of course! We were so proud when the first letter arrived: *Josef Lichtenstein is now bar mitzvah and he read his haphtorah like a true Hasid.*'

Her eyes were the spring blue of the bouquet he had placed at the foot of the shrine behind the vegetable patch, back there, when he had prayed that the little girl, Mila Heller, arrive safely at the home of Zalman Stern. He blinked the shrine away.

'Yes, I knew my haphtorah by heart. We studied during the entire crossing. Reb Halberstamm taught me the meaning of the verses and what they imply besides meaning.'

The last sentence struck her, intense as she remembered him.

'And Williamsburg?' she asked.

'There are people in Williamsburg who remember my parents, and there are people who remember *your* parents: the brilliant scholar Gershon Heller, the beautiful Rachel Landau, may they rest in peace.'

Tears welled in Mila's eyes. Besides the Sterns, no one in Paris could have named her parents.

They knew all that they needed to know about each other in a Hasidic courtship: Blimela, daughter of Rachel, daughter of Haye Esther; Josef, son of Yekutiel, son of Mendel Wolf. And they also knew particulars they should not have known – he, the smell of her hair covered in black earth; she, the taste of his tears.

They looked down at the ivory tablecloth that Hannah had embroidered in the style of back there; they looked down and then, quickly, at each other. They knew that they would have a lifetime in which to tell each other the dance of stories that had placed them at this table, b'shert, *destined*, among the generations.

THE FRONT DOOR closed on Josef.

'I think it is yes!' Hannah cried out. 'B'shert, it is b'shert!' Hannah took Mila by the waist and waltzed her around the dining table. '*Yadidadidam!*'

'Auntie Hannah, the doctor said bed rest!'

They glided through the entrance hall, they stopped in front of Zalman's study. 'Mazel tov!' Hannah cried out.

Zalman's hands came together as he rose. He was beaming. He no longer needed to be afraid, not for this daughter marrying at the Rebbe's court. 'Mazel tov!'

Mila and Josef met two more times before the wedding, but not alone. The first time, Josef brought Mila his mother's brooch and a modest diamond engagement ring. Mila pinned the brooch on the collar of her suit, close to her heart. The second time, he brought her two gift boxes, one white, flat, tied with a purple ribbon; one purple, tied with a white ribbon. Mila pulled on the purple ribbon, unwrapped the fragile rice paper, unfolded a silk stole. She stroked the pearl-and-lavender stripes, but did not bring the fabric to her cheek for fear that it might seem immodest. She pulled the white ribbon, brushed the hand-painted flower on the frosted-blue perfume bottle, and with her light Hungarian lilt, she read out the label: '*Anémone des bois.*'

Josef pulled back his hips and stood a bit hunched, coat closed, to conceal his twenty-two-year-old ammah rising in praise of Mila and HaShem.

AFTER THE ENGAGEMENT, Hannah announced that a bride-to-be needed a room of her own. Mila protested. Like most Hasidic girls, she knew nothing of the intimate inspections that precede a Jewish orthodox wedding night, but after she started private bride classes, Mila moved into the living room. Atara came to visit every evening. She brushed Mila's hair, bristles rustling over the waves and highlights, the long hair Mila and Atara knew would soon lay curled at the bottom of a wastebasket, the long hair Josef would never touch. Their gazes met in the mirror.

Once again, Mila peeled back the folds of the fragile rice paper wrapping Josef's gifts. She stroked the silk stole. 'I'll wear it every month, to let him know when I am permitted,' she said one evening.

'Permitted?' Atara asked, and did not wait for an answer.

Atara did not want to know, did not want any of what she soon understood was Mila's count of blood days and clean days, a count Mila entered in a new notebook she had titled, in her flowing cursive and well-rounded loops: *Mila's Book of Days – Private.*

★

THE MEN sang the groom to the wedding dais with a joyous march: *'There was a king among the righteous ...'* Zalman turned to face the centre aisle, to await the bride, and the guests turned with him. He hummed the melody he had hummed at the wedding of his study partner, Gershon Heller, back there, in Transylvania, *Bilvovi mishkan evneh (In my heart I will build a temple),* he hummed until Gershon's daughter appeared, a white radiance holding a pale bouquet in gathered hands.

Mila could not see where she was stepping, under the thick veil that covered her face, but Hannah and Mrs Halberstamm guided her. When Mila's foot reached the dais, Zalman thundered 'Blessed be she that cometh!', and to the measure of the voice that had been deemed the most beautiful east of Vienna, Mila circled Josef seven times for the seven heavens, the seven days of creation, the seven rotations of the phylactery strap; as man binds himself to God, so Mila would bind herself to Josef.

Josef slid a wedding ring on Mila's finger. He uttered the ancient vow: 'Harei at mekudesheth li b'taba'ath zo kedath Moshe v'Yisroel.' (*Lo thou art consecrated to me with this ring according to the Law of Moses and Israel.*)

Hannah lifted the veil from Mila's face.

There were no blood relations on either side to attend the wedding.

Arm in arm, eyes sparkling, bride and groom stepped down from under the dais.

In winding chains, the men wove their steps on the men's side, the women on the women's side. The dance continued into the night, until a sign from Zalman indicated it was time for the festivities to wind down. What was the propriety of so much joy when the Temple was destroyed, when the divine presence was in exile?

★

MILA LAY in darkness, silence and holiness.

She imagined her long hair, shorn for this night, gathering itself inside her prayer book, inside the night table, just as Anghel's locks had gathered on the newspapers ten years earlier.

Now Josef stood by her bed, swaying in prayer.

She was surprised to find herself within the Law, yet alone with him.

He leaned over her, kissed her cheek.

Between their bodies, his long nightshirt, a few remaining inches of darkness, her gown, which he now lifted.

He held her like milkweed, afraid to crush, afraid his breathing might carry her off.

May our union be in holiness ... May our children ...

She felt his hardness searching for the place in her she barely knew of, until she learned to inspect it in preparation for this night.

Her gasp as he pressed into her. He stilled — was he doing something wrong? He had intended to think of Torah matters, as the sages advised, but his whole being arced towards her.

He felt the pull of her, pressed harder.

Again, she gasped.

His seed in her, his seed in her as in dreams of her but unlike anything he had experienced in waking life.

He stroked her lips, her lashes — he stopped. Bride and groom must separate as soon as the act is consummated. He stumbled out of bed and stood, uncertain, in the dark. When was it permitted to speak again?

'I'm fine,' she whispered.

136

The ache of her tenderness made him almost reach for her, to hold her against his chest where she would hear the beat of *Mila MilaHeller* . . .

'Mila Heller,' he whispered.

'Lichtenstein, now my name is Lichtenstein,' she whispered back.

He pulled up a chair, making sure it did not touch her covers, *And every bed whereon she lieth shall be unclean.* He sat, and they both thought of the hollow in the bluff, back there, where they had clasped each other's hands until dark. It seemed they never had, never would, let go.

At dawn, he was still sitting by her bed. Her scarf had slid from her shorn head and he felt awe and gratitude in front of her beauty. Her eyes flicked open, so big in her unadorned face, and he uttered the first prayer of the day, *'Modeh ani . . . shehechezarta bi nishmati . . .' (I thank Thee . . . for returning my soul within me . . .)*

★

HANNAH now called Atara the next kaleh meidel, the next girl in age of marriage. She took her shopping for kaleh meidel dresses. Atara protested. She did not need such outfits, not yet. Proudly, Hannah handed the saved banknotes to the store owner. 'A Stern girl in age of marriage has a proper wardrobe.'

Atara held back tears.

A few months after Mila's wedding, Atara rose in the middle of the night. She folded her kaleh meidel dress into a bag that she hung on Etti's doorknob.

A toothbrush, some underwear.

The time switch did not tick in the stairwell, she went down in the dark. Zalman's ancient curses echoed from flight to flight:

> *You will fail at whatever you undertake.*
> *You will sink from one depravity to the next.*
> *You will wander the world and never find a home.*

Atara pressed the buzzer that released the latch of the porte cochère that gave onto the street. The heavy oak door half opened. In the shivery Parisian dawn, a swell of poppies swayed, each blossom a scarlet freedom quivering on its fragile stem.

Book III

Williamsburg, Brooklyn

AFTER THE SEVEN DAYS OF CELEBRATION, THE newlyweds boarded a plane to New York. Josef's study partner fetched them at the airport. He gave news of the Rebbe's court, of children born to Josef's yeshiva-mates during Josef's stay in Paris. Mila thought she recognised names from her childhood in Transylvania, names of children who had boarded the cattle cars, names now borne by new children. Outside the station wagon, streetscapes unlike any she had ever known: detached houses set apart by thin voids, not the continuous façades of French towns; outside, the rush of traffic, shriller as buildings rose higher, but inside the car, the familiar names.

A sweep of cables, a bridge suspended, a sharp turn — suddenly, signs in Yiddish and Hebrew: GLATT SUPER-VISION, YETEV LEV SCHOOL FOR BOYS, 100 PERCENT WOOL . . . , kosherness splashed all over, not discreetly indicated as it had been in Paris; Jews not afraid to advertise they were Jews; Jews reconstructing a world that never was before.

Eager to spend their first Sabbath in their own apart-ment, Mila and Josef declined all invitations. Mila pored over the recipes she had written down under Hannah's dictation; Josef peeled carrots and parsnips for the chicken soup. When the smells of Sabbath cooking filled their tiny apartment, Mila and Josef looked at each other with delight – a home, their home.

They bathed and put on their Sabbath clothes. Mila wore the white headdress that Hannah had embroidered with gold thread; Josef wore his fur shtreimel, a wedding present from Zalman. Eighteen minutes before sunset, Mila's hands circled the Sabbath candles, outward then inward, to gather and protect. Eyes closed, she whispered the ancient prayer, *Let these lights anchor me as they have anchored so many before me . . .*, and Mila felt fingers clasping her fingers, a chain of candle-lighting hands reaching from the deep past into the future. When she opened her eyes, the weave of Josef's caftan shimmered like leaves after rain.

He, watching the candles' flames mirrored in the gold edging of Mila's headdress, allowed himself to remember his first mother, her hugs and kisses. 'Gut Shabbes, kleiner Yiddeleh!' (*Good Sabbath, little Jew!*) This time, the memory did not break him.

In her Book of Days, Mila counted five days of blood and seven clean days. During the seven clean days, she wore white underwear and slept on white sheets. Morning and evening, she inserted a white cloth, deep; she turned, retrieved, examined as prescribed. Were she to find a reddish spot, she would have to label the cloth or underwear with the time and day of count: spotting red did not mean spotting pink or brown; only a rabbi could establish whether the tint required longer separation.

Mila was scrupulous about the laws of family purity that checked impulses, enhanced fertility, and assured pure souls for the children to come.

On the seventh clean day, she waited for sundown and went to the ritual bath. She flossed her teeth, filed her nails. She soaped, rinsed. An attending woman would check for any hatzitza (*barrier*), stray hair, smudge that might come between ritual waters and skin.

Mila descended the steps into the small, rectangular pool of *natural* water; water supplied by gravity and not pumped in. Arms extended, eyes and mouth closed but not clenched, she let herself sink.

'Kosher!' the attendant chimed when Mila's head broke the water.

Arms folded below her heart to separate higher realms from lower realms, Mila whispered the blessing for ritual immersion, and two more times, she let herself sink.

'Kosher! Kosher!'

Taking hold of her robe, Mila did feel pure and white and proud to be a Jewish woman whom rabbis could pronounce kosher. And tears flowed down her face, of gratitude to HaShem for guiding her and helping her resist the temptations of Paris.

As the rabbis advised, she put on coloured underwear so she would not notice a slight irregularity on permitted days. Walking home, she hastened her step to reduce the odds of an encounter with an unclean animal, an ignorant person, a Gentile – any encounter that might compromise her chances of conceiving a Torah scholar.

In the bedroom, in front of the three-sided mirror, she

draped her shoulders in the silk stole, pearl grey and lavender in the lamplight, the sign that would convey to Josef that she was permitted, and in the silent room, she thought she could hear her parents pray to live again in the generations Josef and Mila might bring forth.

Josef stood at the foot of Mila's bed. He listened for the soft rustle of the eiderdown as she lifted a corner. At last the light fragrance of *Anémone des bois* on her skin. *May our union* – her thighs under him, opening . . . *grant us to draw holy souls for our children . . .*

This time, they did not separate immediately; only after dam betulim *(hymeneal bleeding)* must bride and groom separate immediately. This time they would not have to separate until she menstruated – if she menstruated.

They lay next to each other in the dark. There were rules prescribing everything up to, and during, but this moment of simply lying together felt entirely unbounded, unruled. She pressed closer to him and his beard felt silken in the night, like her father's beard under the prayer shawl, her father whispering, 'Blimela, my Blimela . . .'

For the next two weeks, Mila rushed to the front door as soon as she heard Josef's step on the landing. Once, she struck up a song, shyly; Mila had not sung in front of a grown male since she was twelve. But Josef was her husband and it was permitted.

'*Oyfn veg, shteyt a boym* – you don't know the words? Repeat after me: *Oy, Mama, I so want to be a bird . . .*' And she led him in her dance. '*Yadiyadidam!*' One raised hand holding one end of the stole, the other arm

144

framing her head, she twirled in the high heels from Paris, and sometimes she brought out the matching handbag from Paris and waved it rhythmically, like a tambourine, from one side of her narrow waist to the other. *'Yadidadam!'* Josef's heart beat faster. In the high heels, Mila's ankles seemed so delicate, her calf elongated—

'Josef! Come, dance!'

He loved her capacity to emerge from seriousness into coquetry, and most of all he loved the lilt of her voice, the Hungarian inflections. He stomped in. They sashayed facing each other, from dining table to couch, eyes shining in the tiny apartment.

ON NIGHTS of separation, they talked in their parallel beds. Josef told Mila about the ship to America thumping onward, always onward, while behind were the unfinished goodbyes. 'I wanted to go back, to explain . . . explain what? I *had* stepped out of the undergrowth, I *had* spoken to the Jew. Every morning, I stood on the deck wiping sea mist from my lashes. Reb Halberstamm pulled me back, led me to the cabin, to the open book. That's why I was ready for my bar mitzvah. Even when the ship pulled into the New York harbour and all the passengers stood on the deck, turned towards the Statue of Liberty, we went back to our cabin and rehearsed my haphtorah. When we disembarked, Reb Halberstamm told me not to look right or left: "What is there to see in the treifenah medinah, the unkosher land of modernity?" I did look, of course . . .' Josef went quiet. He did not tell Mila that during the journey from the ship landing to Hasidic Williamsburg, his heart vaulted when the car drove by a cross, on a street corner, that his hand came to his pocket, to the postcard he would mail to Florina as soon as he had ploughed the fields of America and could send for her.

When Josef started again, he said, 'In Williamsburg, Reb Halberstamm led me past half-open doors, rooms where boys singsonged words I could almost remember, *And God spoke to Moses* . . . I saw Jewish boys raise their hands and fidget on their seats to answer the teacher's question, Jewish boys who did not fear to be first in their class. At services, men pinched my cheek. "Fine lineage Josef, son of Yekutiel, son of Mendel Wolf." The men thought they knew who I was, they seemed to think it was a good thing to be Josef Lichtenstein, son of Yekutiel, son of Mendel Wolf, grandnephew of Rebbe Elimelech . . .

'I wasn't used to being surrounded by so many boys, boys dressed liked Jews . . . I struggled with my skullcap, with being indoors all the time. I went for long walks. I missed the orchards, the geese, the smell of upturned soil. I missed . . .'

'Florina? You missed Florina?'

There was a long pause before Josef started again. 'Then one day, walking along Lee Avenue, I realised *I* was the Jewish boy who followed me in every window, *I* was the boy with sidecurls who mimicked my every move. That day, at services, my voice joined the men's voices and I, too, asked that my dead rise, that they rise whole. And I asked for Mila Heller's dead, too.'

'You thought of me then, Josef?'

On another night of separation, Mila asked, 'Do you write to Florina? Why don't you write?'

'Because I am lost to her.'

'She would still want to hear from you.'

'She would want to hear from Anghel, not Josef.'

'She understands you had to go back to your people.'

Josef did not reply. He saw, in the mist of the Nadăş River, Florina reach for the boy with the wood-nettle eyes, he saw her hand fall to her side, empty.

The next day, Mila prepared her first package for Florina: canned fruit, coffee, sugar, a wrinkle-free apron, a wool sweater. She was placing inside the package a folded, flowery silk fabric when Josef asked, 'What is it for?'

'A beautiful dress,' Mila said.

'But Florina wears black.'

'Even now she wears black?'

Josef let out a heavy sigh.

Determinedly, Mila arranged the flowered silk inside the package.

In the post office, waiting in line for the postage to Romania, Mila wrote her new name and her Williamsburg address on a postcard. Not knowing Atara's address, she took the card home and placed it between two pages of her Book of Days.

★

On the Festival of the Law, Simchath Torah, Mila and Josef attended services at the main synagogue. Mila was still enchanted by this world in which everyone was dressed as she and Josef were dressed, women in white kerchiefs, men in shtreimels. People she had never met greeted them as if they were reuniting; some had known her parents, some remembered her as a toddler, and the newlyweds walked with a greater sense of purpose – they, too, would raise a name in Israel for their murdered parents and siblings.

In front of the synagogue, Josef pointed to a side door. 'The women's entrance. Don't be shy. Push to the front row or you won't see a thing.'

A swell of white kerchiefs rolled upward, a surge Mila hoped would sweep her along, but kept leaving her behind. Her neighbour recognised the young bride from Paris and took hold of Mila's elbow. Together they thrust themselves up the stairs, to the front row.

Unlike the balcony in the Paris synagogue, where a low screen of bronze rosettes allowed men on the main floor to crane their necks and wave to their wives, the women's balcony in the Williamsburg synagogue was set behind a high, tightly woven wooden lattice. Mila pressed an eye to a diamond-shaped opening in the lath. The first round had begun. The men's feet lifted and fell rhythmically. She looked for Josef but could not find him in a crowd of hundreds dressed as he was, in shimmering black caftans and sable-fur hats.

In the centre of the circle, wearing a white caftan, the Rebbe swayed, cradling a small Torah scroll. His prayer shawl draped over his head and covered his face. The Rebbe ran a few steps as if borne aloft by the men's singing; the men receded like reeds. 'Aye mamale mamale aye,' the Rebbe cried out. 'Ayeyaiyaiyaiyai!' his Hasidim responded.

Watching the men dance, it was as if Mila, too, were dancing; hearing the men sing, it was as if she, too, were singing, and when the Rebbe leapt, hugging the scroll to his chest, the tingling in Mila's knees spread to her belly.

The Rebbe raised the Torah scroll; the two lions embroidered on the scroll's mantle advanced, retreated, and pranced along the circle, their front paws upholding Judah's crown.

The Rebbe's head rolled from side to side and his prayer shawl slid down to his shoulders.

His face uncovered, Mila recognised him at once: the man with the high forehead, loose sidecurls, deep eye sockets; the man who kept looking into a book when her mother ran to him – the man in the open boxcar.

Women behind her jostled to get a glimpse, prying her away from the lattice, but Mila's hands clenched the slats. Her neighbour spoke in Mila's ear: 'See how the light shines *from* his face, not *on* his face!'

The Rebbe ran a few steps, away from her, then he turned back and Mila thought he was running towards her, dancing in front of her as he chanted *'Aye mamale aye …'* The Rebbe circled away, twisting this way, that way, like a flame, and inside this flame Mila saw the vanishing train, and she, reaching this way, that way, for her mother and father, reaching, reaching—

Mama? She held out a hand to a shadow on the ceiling;

her other hand clung, white-knuckled, to the lattice. Her knees folded under her and she felt her balance slip. Just when the synagogue grew quiet for the Rebbe to sing, Mila called aloud 'Mama? Rebbe?' and slumped to the floor.

Josef heard the cry; he heard the commotion in the balcony.

'It's all right, she's coming to,' someone said when he tore open the door to the women's stairway.

Mila appeared at the top of the stairs, leaning on two women.

Josef helped her out of the synagogue.

The dancing resumed in the main hall, while the women in the mezzanine already wondered about the young bride from Paris: A female raising her voice in public, in the Rebbe's presence? A fragile health, God forbid . . .

When Mila lay tucked under her eiderdown, Josef asked what had happened.

'Of course it was him,' Mila said, 'that was why we went, to see the Rebbe dance.'

'You saw the Rebbe before?'

'My father held me up during an entire sermon so I would see the Rebbe's face. How would I forget his fiery eyes as he threatened, begged, wept, as he warned against Zionism? Then I saw him again . . . Josef, what do people here say of the Rebbe's escape?'

'A miracle. There is a big celebration every year, the twenty-first of Kislev, the anniversary date of his arrival in Switzerland. We'll go. The whole community goes.'

'No one asks how the Rebbe found himself on that train for *prominenten*?'

'The man who negotiated the train had a dream: You must take the Rebbe of Szatmár or your mission will not succeed.'

'A dream? That's how the Rebbe found himself on the train to Switzerland?'

'Everyone in Williamsburg knows about it.'

'Yes?' Mila's hands tapped the eiderdown. 'No one wonders why this one train ended up in Switzerland and not in Auschwitz? It's all right Josef, I'm fine. I'm glad the Rebbe escaped . . . but it's all true, isn't it? The things that happened to me really happened to me? The open boxcars, my mother running, yelling, *"Rebbe!"*?'

'You mustn't think of it . . . or when you do think of it, think of us, our future, our future children.'

'I will. I will. Now go back to shul. You must. People will talk if you miss another round – Josef? Please bring me my T'nach. Tonight we read the passage about Moses not crossing into the promised land, right?' Again, she tapped the eiderdown. 'Go now, go. I'm fine.'

Mila opened her Book of Scripture. In keeping with the tradition on Simchath Torah, Mila read from the end of the Book of Scripture to the beginning,

> *Thou shalt not go over thither. So Moses died . . .*
> *and the children of Israel wept . . . and there arose not*
> *a prophet since . . . in all the great terror which Moses*
> *showed in the sight of all Israel.*
>
> *In the Beginning . . .*

★

IN HER BOOK OF DAYS, Mila counted: *Blood: 1, 2 … 5. Clean: 1, 2, 3 … 7.*

She draped her shoulders in the silver and purple stole.

When there was blood again, at the end of the month, she wanted to curl up and be consoled by Josef, but she knew the yearning was a manifestation of her evil inclination. Why else would she ache for his arms precisely during the part of the month when they could not touch? He could not blow a feather off her dress, *lest it lead to transgression.*

EVERY MONTH, Mila went to the ritual bath, but her belly did not swell.

It was not a good thing for a young woman in Williamsburg not to be pregnant.

There was not much to be, in Williamsburg, for a woman who was not pregnant.

From her window in the breezeless apartment, Mila watched the pram-pushing mothers trailed by lines of hand-holding children, the youngest closest to the pram. She could almost make out the plump baby knuckles squeezing the metal tubing. *Next month, dear Lord, let it be me.*

BLOOD DAYS, clean days, on every corner a neighbour's belly pushed against the fabric of a skirt, one more Hasid impatient to undo the terrible destruction. *Next month, dear Lord, remember me.*

.   .   .

When Mila passed among them, women hushed their talk of baby bottles and nappies. At Sabbath services, they held on to her hand. 'I'm praying for you, Mrs Lichtenstein.' The women buried their faces in their Scriptures; their torsos swayed. *He That maketh the barren wife to be a joyful mother . . .*

During the third year of their marriage, Mila consulted with her neighbours, who recommended a physician in Manhattan.

'The doctor says twenty-one is still young,' Mila told Josef upon her return. 'He doesn't see anything wrong.'
'Of course there's nothing wrong,' Josef said.

On the High Holy Days, Mila prayed with heightened fervour. *Tekiah!* the horn summoned; *Teruah*, the horn wailed, and Mila pleaded: *Inscribe our child, O Lord, in the Book of Life.*
Josef, too, prayed for children. He never expressed disappointment, but at night, he dreamt of her fullness. How lovely she was in those dreams, her belly rounded, her thin face filled in. He dreamt of her singing to the child, *Yadidadidam!*

THEY HAD PLANNED for Josef to study *until the children came*, but the children kept not coming and Josef was turning into a fixture in the House of Study. Alone in the small apartment, Mila gazed at the hard spines of Josef's Talmud set. On occasion, she opened a tome: a lot of Aramaic, which she did not decipher as well as Hebrew. She picked up the more familiar Expanded Rabbinic

Bible, which she read as she had been taught to read in Zalman's home and at the seminary, stopping after each word, each cluster of words, for the rabbinic interpretations that unveiled the text's meaning. But as her melancholy grew, Mila paused less frequently for the gloss's smaller, fainter typeface. What exegesis did Mila need to grasp Rachel's plea, *Give me a child or I will die.*

Except for Hannah's needlepoint of a stag with large antlers near a watering hole, the walls were bare, as were the walls in most Hasidic homes. A glass leaf shielded the glossy tabletop, a wedding present from the Halberstamms, for when the children came.

Evening fell. She looked out the living-room window. She tried to make out Josef's coat among the men rushing on the overpass. In Paris, Josef had stood out, his garb exotic, his black hat sacerdotal, and she had seen that he was handsome, the man who came from the land of her torn childhood, but among the scores of black flaps scuttling on the overpass, she could not distinguish his coat. She picked up her embroidery of the Tomb of Rachel, who had so begged for a child and had been granted two — *Mother Rachel, show me the healing leaves.*

★

'THE DOCTOR says twenty-two is young. There's nothing wrong.'

'Of course twenty-two is young,' Josef said.

★

EVERY TWO YEARS, Mila and Josef returned to Paris for Passover with the Sterns. As if her former home might restore her former promise, Mila filled with a child's enchantment when the taxi drove along the yew hedges of the Tuileries, along the elms always budding at that season. At last, the taxi turned the corner with the familiar street sign, white letters on a marine background: RUE DE SÉVIGNÉ. Mila's hand lingered on the quarter-turn of the handrail that used to slow her when she slid down, chest against wax-scented walnut. She ran up the three flights. The burnished mezuzah on the door-post, the doorsill, and into Hannah's arms. After the joy of reunion, after tea and cake, Mila asked, 'May I? Now?'

Hannah smiled. 'Go child, go.'

The heavy porte cochère swung open. Mila gazed up

and down the street. Limestone mouldings, wrought-iron scrolls, peeling wooden shutters all felt precious after the bland functionality of Williamsburg. Her arm extended to feel the old wall's caress. A note escaped from the violin repair shop. Snippets of conversation from passers-by; her ear harkened after the longed-for liaisons, the vowels softened by *l*'s and *z*'s and velvety *t*'s, the steady cadences that strummed the lives of those who do not leave.

In the Luxembourg Gardens, she followed the chestnut-lined alley to the playground of her childhood, the shady coves of her adolescence. At every bend, she half expected Atara to appear. *Best friends, sisters for life.*

When Hannah and Zalman had found Atara's note, Zalman hired detectives to bring her home, but the detectives failed to find her. Mila had witnessed Zalman and Hannah's worry and despair. She had witnessed the stunned younger siblings in front of their parents' wretchedness. When Zalman decreed that Atara's name would not be spoken in the household, Mila did not protest. But despite Zalman's pronouncement, during every Passover visit, Hannah whispered to Mila, 'Have you heard anything?'

Mila thought of Atara's postcards to Hannah. Always the same three words: *I am fine.* Once: *My chère Maman, Please do not worry about me.*

Mila understood why Atara was not reaching out to her – how would Mila face Hannah and Zalman if she became an accessory to their daughter's escape?

Mila stopped by the Fontaine de Médicis. Under the tall, untrimmed plane trees reflected in the dark pool, she gazed, briefly, at the forbidden human representations, the marble tangle of limb and voluptuousness, the nymph surrendering in her lover's lap – and turned her eyes away. She took the exit across the rue Servandoni, looped through the Place Saint-Sulpice to the rue de Seine, and down to the Pont des Arts.

She leaned against the bridge's railing. The sky meandered in the river that, unlike her, could roam far while tarrying, languorously, in Paris. Ribbons of windows and mansard roofs framed the embankments; here, there, spires, cupolas; she wanted to arch over the domes and bend over the bridges and wrap her limbs around the bulbous balusters. The bells rang the quarter hour, the half hour.

When her shadow grew long, she headed home and threw herself into the frantic Passover cleaning where not one crumb, not one speck of leavened bread must remain. The swirl of Hannah's growing family intensified Mila's exertion. She doted on Hannah's latest-born, changed the baby, cooed to it.

At last Passover came and the cleaning could stop.

During the Passover Seder, Mila loved Zalman's re-enactment of the Hebrews' flight from Egypt. Zalman paced the dining room, a satchel of unleavened bread on his shoulder. 'This is how our ancestors fled the land where we were slaves ...' She loved that Zalman still turned to her to welcome the prophet Elijah. In the dark entry, she held her breath as she opened the door.

'Blessed be he who cometh!' Zalman bellowed from the dining room.

She tried to make out Elijah's silhouette in the dark, empty stairwell.

Passover mornings, she went to synagogue; afternoons, she accompanied the children to the Luxembourg Gardens. In a daze of spring, bright skies, and flowering urns, she pushed the baby carriage and watched over the toddlers. An infant's cry or babble would call up her empty apartment in Williamsburg, its windows and tabletop clear of baby fingerprints. She slapped her flat belly: *Why?*

The children followed her home, silent.

★

EACH RETURN to Williamsburg grew more difficult. The fourth year of her marriage, climbing out of the taxi, Mila no longer marvelled at the bold Yiddish and Hebrew signs but wondered how she had not noticed, upon her first arrival, the trash cans punctuating the stoops, the garbage spilling onto the pavements. She almost wished she had forgone the trip to France, it was followed by such longing. Cars honked in the sunken roadway and Mila ached for bells pealing time in melancholy or joy, for deserted August in Paris, and September with its rustle of fresh beginnings in fallen leaves . . .

And every month, the count of blood and despair.

Her reflection in the mirror riled her; her beauty exasperated her. Breasts empty of milk! Arms empty of child! Pleas tumbled from her lips, to barren women in Israel, *Mother Sarah, Mother Rivka, how I thirst for the breath of my baby!*

THE FIFTH YEAR of their marriage, Mila told Josef that her physician insisted on a semen sample before prescribing fertility drugs.

'But it is a grievous sin,' Josef replied. 'The Torah forbids it.'

'Even for medical purposes? The doctor says some of his orthodox patients did do the test.'

'Our Rebbe would never permit it.'

'Even for couples who cannot have children?'

'Mila, how would the doctor help if the problem lies with me?'

'But if the problem *doesn't* lie with you, then the doctor will prescribe fertility drugs.'

'The Torah itself forbids it, not just rabbinic law. No

God-fearing rabbi would permit it.' He hesitated. 'Many women have been helped by the Rebbe's blessing.'

'You ask him. I won't go to the Rebbe.'

★

LEAFING THROUGH magazines in the doctor's waiting room, the name *Kasztner* leapt off a page. Mila's heart beat faster. A book had been published about Kasztner's train for *prominenten*. The magazine slipped from her lap – Josef was right, it was better not to think about those times. She rose and asked the receptionist how much longer it would be, but as the wait continued, her hand reached for the magazine. She read the review, and buried the magazine at the bottom of a stack of *Expectant Mother*s.

Her heart felt heavy when she left the doctor's office. She walked past the subway entrance, and kept walking. She stopped in front of the Forty-Second Street public library.

Face flushed, she climbed the grand stairway. The serenity of the long reading room unsettled her. How could a place where men and women mingled, how could a den of heresy, present such a tranquil front?

The reference librarian directed her to a historical atlas of Central Europe. Mila's finger traced the border that had divided Transylvania during World War II; her finger traced the parallel blue line of the Nadăş River, which she had crossed on her father's shoulders; traced the thin, black railway line that, near Kolozvár, almost touched the war border. To the north: Hungary; to the south: Romania. And there, in tiny print on the river's bend, *Deseu*, where Anghel had lived with Florina. Indeed, a train from Kolozvár to Budapest could have gone – would have gone – past the shed where she and her parents had been hiding.

From then on, Mila returned to the Forty-Second Street library every time she had an appointment with her physician. Mila had been taught that Atara's insistence on finding out what happened was a *pleasure-seeking* quest, a toying with superficial matters instead of the weightier teachings of the Law, but now Mila recognised that whatever was driving her own need to return to the library, Atara must have felt from a young age.

Watching a clerk retrieve books from a rolling cart, watching the clerk shelve the books, Mila imagined Atara working in such a place, that one day Atara would appear behind the reference desk. Finally Mila summoned the nerve to ask the woman behind the checkout counter if she knew someone named Atara Stern, who particularly liked libraries. The woman politely explained that the New York Public Library had many thousands of patrons.

In the reading room, as the light travelled across the tall windows, Mila came across an article by a professor at City University, Fifth Avenue. She realised the address was near the library. She walked down the few blocks and found him in a small office behind a glass door. Yes, the Kasztner train was a subject of deep interest to him, both as a historian and because he owed his life to Kasztner: the professor's mother was pregnant with him when she escaped on Kasztner's train. Yes, he knew about the Satmarer Rebbe's escape. He had documents, testimonies . . .

ONE THURSDAY evening, Josef was peeling carrots for the Sabbath soup when Mila said, 'About the dream, about Kasztner's dead mother, or his aide's dead mother urging Kasztner, or his aide, to rescue the Rebbe of Szatmár — is that how the Rebbe explains his escape?'

'I believe it was the Rebbe himself who told the story of the dream but I never heard him talk of it.'

'Some people are angry with the Rebbe. They say he, and other community leaders who fled on that train, behaved shamefully. They say these leaders knew about the camps, knew that Kasztner's train would be let out only if other Jews did not resist deportation. That's why Kasztner's convoy left Kolozvár after the other Jews were deported: to make sure the *prominenten* remained silent. "It was a good bargain," Eichmann said during his trial.'

'What are you talking about?'

'Kolozvár was only four kilometres from the border and Jews were no longer killed in Romania in the spring of '44. Had the Jews of Kolozvár known about the extermination camps, they would have fled. There were twenty thousand Jews and a handful of armed guards. Some would have been shot while fleeing, but most would have survived.'

'What do you mean, "Had they known about the camps"? No one knew.'

'The leaders had been warned. Certainly our Rebbe knew enough to escape with the help of a Zionist even though he had expelled from the congregation anyone who interacted with Zionists.'

'The Rebbe never asked a Zionist for help. He never asked to be on that train.'

'He *begged.* "Nem mir, Ich bin der Rebbe of Szatmár."' (*Take me, I am the Rebbe of Szatmár.*)

'Nem mir?' Josef laughed. 'Our Rebbe asked to be part of a venture negotiated by a Zionist?'

'*Begged.* And Josef, our Rebbe would never have transgressed the Sabbath if he had not known it was a question of life and death. He knew, Josef, he knew about the extermination camps—'

'Our Rebbe transgressed the Sabbath?'

'Atara told me years ago. She read it in newspapers. There was a trial . . . I didn't want to think of it . . . I went to the library.'

'You went inside a library?'

'I had to know, Josef. What if the Rebbe knew what would happen to everyone left behind? What if he did what he accuses Zionists of doing, what if he failed to warn his community—'

'Mila! Where are you hearing such things?'

'I'm not angry with the Rebbe for surviving; I'm angry because when it came to his life, he allowed himself to compromise, but when it comes to our lives, we cannot do the one test that would permit me to start a fertility treatment.'

'It's the test you're talking about? I told you, this isn't about the Rebbe. No God-fearing rabbi would permit what is expressly forbidden in the Torah.'

MILA'S NEIGHBOUR recommended a physician who would prescribe fertility drugs without a semen sample: drugs to regulate Mila's time of ovulation – which had not been irregular – drugs to stimulate her ovaries though everything indicated she ovulated regularly. The drugs, the temperature charts, the count of blood days and clean days, the intimate inspections melded into one wrenching failure to conceive. Mila barely noticed Josef reaching for her, his longing, his tenderness, his embrace.

Clean: 1, 2, 3, 4, 5, 6, 7.

Blood.

Again, she curled up on the bed.

Josef ached to take her in his arms. Nothing wrong with her, the doctors said. Shame swept over him, for her bloated ankles, her nausea, her despair. If he were the infertile one, then she was taking the drugs for naught – the drugs that so altered her moods. He never did deserve her, her tenderness, her beauty that now, too, begged for salvation. He hungered for her laugh, how long it had been since she had pulled him into her dance – *Yadidadidam!*

★

MILA KNEW that after ten years of barren marriage, an orthodox Jew may not abstain any longer from keeping the command to *be fruitful and multiply*. One evening, she asked, 'Almost ten years since we are married. Has anyone suggested . . . that you divorce?'

'Divorce!'

'It is a commandment for a man to bear children.'

He stroked her face, kissed her eyelids. 'You've been taking these drugs too long. Would you consider—'

'I won't stop the fertility treatment.'

Josef reached for a Talmud treatise, searched for a clause that might permit a semen analysis, and once more failed to find it:

> *If his hand touches his penis, let his hand be cut off on his belly.*
> *Would not his belly be split? It is preferable that his belly be split...*
> *If a thorn stuck in his belly, should he not remove it? No.*
> *... But all such, why?*
> *To emit seed in vain is akin to murder.*

★

ON THEIR tenth anniversay, Mila copied out for the first time the verses that weighed so heavily on their marriage, the passage from Genesis about Onan's death sentence for spilling his seed upon the ground. Her handwriting started off steady, intent on making a faithful transcription, but later, as she copied out the verses again and again, the script trembled as she grasped that the story was not Onan's – Onan dies as soon as he is mentioned; the story was Tamar's. Law and custom demanded that Onan's widow, Tamar, be married to Onan's brother, but her father-in-law, Judah, reneged on his promise to do so. Facing childlessness, Tamar took matters into her own hands.

Once more, Mila copied the verses into her Book of Days:

> *And it was told Tamar, saying, Behold thy father-in-law goeth up to Timnath to shear his sheep ... and Tamar took off the garments of her widowhood ... and she sat near the entrance to Enayim, which is on the way to Timnath ... Judah saw her and he thought her to be a harlot ... and he said, 'I pray thee, let me come in unto you ...' And he came in unto her. And she conceived.*

On another evening of separation – Josef was hunched over a Talmud tome at the cleared dining table, Mila was reading her Expanded Rabbinic Bible in the armchair by the window – Mila asked, 'What does it mean, that Tamar sat at Enayim? Was there really a place called *Eyes*?'

'Ah, you too are reading about Onan.'

'About Tamar. The verse says: Tamar sat *bepetach Enayim.*'

166

'One reading is: Tamar sat near the *gate of Two Fountains*. Of course, since *enayim* also means *eyes*, and *petach* also means *opening*, it is not incorrect to read: Tamar sat at, near, the *Eyes' Opening*. The Targum Jonathan says: She sat near a division of paths, near a crossroad that requires all eyes to open and consider which way to proceed.'

'And King David stems from Tamar?'

'So will the messiah. Before Judah knew Tamar, he pledged a signet ring to her. The Midrash says the signet bore a lion to signify that from this union would come the royal line of Israel, the lion of Judah.'

Mila circled back to a commentary and entered it into her notebook:

For a holy mission to succeed, it is sometimes necessary to trick Satan into thinking a holy act is like himself: satanic. It is sometimes necessary to shroud a holy act in sin. So did Rebecca, Jacob, Judah, Tamar ... Rebecca and Jacob deceived Isaac. Jacob married two sisters. Tamar lay with her father-in-law, yet Tamar brought forth the line of King David of whom it is said:

BEHOLD, DAVID WAS ENTIRELY HANDSOME TO
  LOOK AT,
OF ALL HUMANS, DAVID WAS MOST FAVOURED BY
  THE LORD.

Below this, Mila wrote and circled two words:

Nem mir (*take me*)

Two words with which Mila drew the unholy train into the story, and from that moment on, it was all connected in Mila's mind, all the same story: Tamar, Judah, the Rebbe, each shrouding a holy act in the satanic cloak.

The numerologies that had so enchanted Mila at the seminary now spilled from the margins of Scripture into her Book of Days as she attempted her own sums and interpretations.

ותהר, vetahar (*and she conceived*), summed to 611, which summed to → 6 + 1 + 1 = 8.

Eight children?

עינים, enayim, summed to 740, which summed to → 7 + 4 + 0 = 11 → 1 + 1 = 2.

Two children? If she opened her eyes and saw what the Lord wanted her to see, she might have two children? Two was not as many as the other women in Williamsburg, yet how grateful she would be.

But perhaps she should sum bepetach Enayim? Or, better, *petach* only since *be* was a mere preposition? Petach summed to 488 → 4 + 8 + 8 = 20 → 2.

If she sat near the Gate to Enayim, she would have two children? No, they would remain two, the two of them, alone . . .

In the long hours in the empty apartment, amidst her count of blood and clean days, Mila summed and summed again. Sometimes the letters added to 8, 4, 2 . . .

Mila's reading had turned into a desperate burrowing, the verses in Genesis no longer Scripture and Law, but a story, the story she needed to survive − her story. By day, she bore into the words to bring her womb to life; by night, she held on to Tamar's hand so that even in sleep she would not let go of it.

1968

Paris

THE TENTH YEAR OF THEIR MARRIAGE, MILA AND Josef returned to Paris for Passover with the Sterns. During the flight, Mila gazed at the magazines the stewardess handed out: pictures of Martin Luther King shot dead, of a war in Vietnam, pictures of riots in Paris, women going out into the street, taking matters into their hands . . . like Tamar.

Enayim → 2. Petach → 2.

And Paris?

פאריז (*Paris*) → 298 → 2 + 9 + 8 = 19 → 1 + 9 = 10 → 1 + 0 = 1.

One child? If she sat near Enayim in Paris, if she opened her eyes might she have one child?

Policemen in riot gear stopped the taxi near the city centre. Mila explained that her family lived in the Marais, off the rue de Rivoli. The police waved them on. The car inched its way between indigo vans with darkened windows. Placards were plastered on every façade, on traffic signs, bus shelters, bold swatches of scarlet and black, and the slogans of spring 1968 would soon find their way into Mila's notebook:

LE DROIT DE VIVRE NE SE MENDIE PAS, IL
SE PREND
(*don't beg for the right to live, take it*)

ON NE MATRAQUE PAS L'IMAGINATION
(*imagination cannot be hacked*)

And, in every margin:

BEHOLD, DAVID WAS ENTIRELY HANDSOME TO
LOOK AT, OF ALL HUMANS, DAVID WAS MOST
FAVOURED BY THE LORD.

The taxi turned the corner, RUE DE SÉVIGNÉ. Mila
ran up the three flights, into Hannah's arms. After tea
and cake, Mila asked, 'May I? Now?', but Hannah did not
answer the usual, 'Go child, go.' Instead, she explained:
'The streets aren't safe, the Goyim are protesting each
other. You mustn't go out.'

Mila stepped onto the balcony. A black flag rippled on
a roof. Further off, two red flags. Sirens wailed, insistent.
Josef joined Mila. He wanted to use this moment alone to
tell her that he had resolved to consult a rabbi in Paris,
one more lenient than the Rebbe, a rabbi who might
consider allowing the semen sample.

Mila was staring at a poster on the opposite façade.

'*Nous sommes tous des juifs allemands,*' she read out.
'We are all German Jews.'

'What do they mean?' Josef asked.

'Perhaps . . . they want to undo the past. Look, that
poster over there, it's the same face. It says: *Libérez Cohn-
Bendit.* I don't know what it means. Perhaps they want to
repair the world?'

'Josef, have you seen this baraita?' Zalman called from the study. 'The Yismach Moshe says . . .'

Mila and Josef stepped back inside. Josef did not get to tell Mila his latest thoughts regarding the test. Mila lifted Hannah's youngest, inhaled the baby scent, then in a sudden burst, she put down the toddler, opened the front door of the apartment, pulled it shut behind her, and bolted down the stairs.

The demonstration was dammed on the Left Bank. The bridges were barred, the Pont Louis-Philippe and the Pont Marie, but Mila wanted to see, feel this unrest that throbbed as her own. She ran south and across the Pont de Sully, then north towards the boulevard Saint-Michel. A policeman stopped her.

'Ma p'tite dame! Il faut rentrer chez vous!'

In her pink suit with pearl-grey piping, her pearl-grey pillbox hat, this woman did not belong in the Latin Quarter, not on this day, not with the riots.

Mila rose on her toes, to see past the policeman's shoulder, to better hear the students' chant.

The truncheon started to swing.

'Mila!'

She spun around.

Gasping Josef, who had sensed her departure and had run after her. She saw Josef's lips move, but amidst a siren and waves of shouting, she could not hear him. She thought that he must be saying: *But we are holy. Separate. Our concern is God's six hundred and thirteen commandments—*

With a speed that surprised her and the police, she turned and plunged past the cordon. Josef tried to follow, but the tips of two truncheons pressed against his chest.

'Mila!' Josef yelled. The truncheons pressed harder against his chest.

The pillbox hat bobbed up, down, past the tight weave of the marine police jackets.

'Mila! Mila! Mila!'

A ROLLING, delirious tentacle lifted her, carried her forward. Fists pummelled the air in anger and exhilaration. 'C-R-S S-S!' the students chanted. Mila's own arm went up. Her voice, not to be heard in public, not in front of men other than her husband, surged − exquisite melting of boundaries, her timbre mixed with other timbres, as she teetered from raised fist to raised fist, and louder her forbidden voice, 'C-R-S S-S!'

JOSEF STEPPED BACK from the police cordon. He rushed to one side street, then another. All access points to the demonstration were blocked. *Please, Mila, it isn't safe. You're suffering. I've been trying to tell you, I'm thinking of it ... the forbidden test ...* Pushed by a throng, he stumbled into an open door. Out of breath, disoriented, he sat on a bench. *Not in my merit but in theirs, in the name of Abraham Isaac Jacob, dear Lord, preserve from harm Blimela, daughter of Rachel, shield her body, guard her soul ...*

Had she run off because they had entered the tenth year of their barren marriage? Did she fear he might abandon her? Was she trying to risk her life?

When Josef lifted his head, he saw before him blue, shimmering folds that were at once the blue taffeta suit Mila wore the day they met again, across the dining table on the rue de Sévigné, and the folds of Mary's robe—But he was in a church! His arms flailed as if entangled in Mary's billowing mantle, his hand struck the stone stoup, which, through the prism of his anguish and past losses, was the stoup in which Florina wet two fingers to sprinkle his forehead with holy water . . . *To live Anghel, to live.*

THE PROTESTERS were now marching thirty abreast, arms linked behind a row of red flags and black flags. A song erupted, carried by thousands: *'Debout les damnés de la terre!'* Mila did not know the words of the 'Internationale', but she heard the summons to rise up. Then she heard the rumbling boots, as did the students next to her. She leaned into the line and passed cobble after cobble, towards the front, where they flew against shields and helmets. A group broke in from a side street. *'Libérez nos camarades!'* Mila started her own rally cry: 'E-na-yim!' A teenager waving a black flag took up her chant: 'U-na-nimes! U-na-nimes!' Mila's eyes teared from acrid, whistling smoke. A rush threw her to the ground. A swinging club – too close, the seam of her skirt ripped, her wig and hat swivelled, askew one instant, then gone . . . arms pulling her, lifting her, helping her up . . . a winding stair, a terrace overlooking smoke and flashes—

'A disinfectant! Bandage!'

A youth unwound the red scarf from his neck and knelt at her feet. Mila's eyes opened wide on the scarlet thread:

> . . . *And it came to pass in the time of Tamar's travail, and behold . . . the one put out his hand and the midwife bound upon his hand a scarlet thread . . .*

After swaddling the cut on her heel, the youth ran his fingers through the stubble on her head. 'Like the Brancusi muse: smooth and perfectly whole. Perfectly beautiful.'

Mila understood that her wig was gone; she flushed, deeply.

'Comrades!' the youth called, extending an arm towards her.

'Revolution est belle,' someone whispered.

Mila's arms lifted; her hands covered her scalp as she hobbled towards the stairs.

'Don't!' the students cried out.

The youth's hand on her shoulder, holding her back. 'The bastards club anyone they come across after a demonstration.'

'I must,' Mila said.

'I'll go with you.'

'No!' she replied abruptly, thinking of Josef's and Zalman's shock if they saw her next to a sheigets. 'I mean . . . stay with the protests. I can get home.'

The youth hesitated.

'Please!' she begged.

He stepped back. 'Don't forget, tomorrow 15:00 hours in front of the Sorbonne. Wear flat shoes, it's easier to escape. À demain!' He kissed her left cheek, her right cheek.

She hopped down the stairs, one hand on the railing, the other hand where his lips had met her skin. She stepped into the lane and remained very still as the breeze brushed her scalp that had been covered ten years. She removed the red scarf from her foot and tied it around her head. Limping down the street, she heard the students call from the terrace: 'Your name! Xavier here wants to know your name!'

· · ·

JOSEF WAS PACING the half-lit entryway. He could hear the children call from the balcony, 'Mila! Josef!' He wondered whether he would have to tell Hannah she had lost yet another daughter when the porte cochère opened.

There Mila stood, a rag around her head, her skirt unseamed, shoeless. 'I'm fine,' she was saying. 'Please run up and get my other wig. In the black suitcase. Quick!'

Josef hurried up the stairs but the door opened before he rang the bell; the children on the balcony had seen Mila. Hannah came running down. She clasped her hands in grief and disbelief. 'HaShem yerachem (*the Lord have mercy*), where is your wig?'

'It's my fault,' Josef said. 'We got caught in the melee.'

'Why, why did you go out?'

'We . . . I was curious,' Josef said. 'I didn't know it would be – like this.'

And this was the first time that Josef lied for Mila.

France went on strike. The police occupied the Sorbonne, then left; the students occupied the Sorbonne, the streets quieted down, but after her foray in the riot, the night of their arrival in Paris, Mila stayed home. Surely the feeling of connection to the world outside, that she had experienced the night of the riot, was a trick of her evil inclination. She prayed for a Torah fortress – concrete walls, not metaphor – to intercept the chants and slogans.

The days wore on. The return to Williamsburg neared and Josef grew desperate. He had placed such hope in the trip to Paris, but in Paris, too, Mila would not leave the apartment. 'The streets are safe now,' he pleaded, 'go to the Luxembourg, the Palais Royal.' She shook her head, no. He asked whether it would help if he accompanied her, but he did not insist; he sensed she felt slightly embarrassed next to him, when people stared – with his sidecurls and black coat, they turned into objects of curiosity in the streets of Paris. 'Won't you take the children out?' Always, Mila shook her head. 'We're leaving in two weeks.' 'One week.' 'We're leaving in five days.' She shook her head, no.

The impending return to Williamsburg brought the scrawling in Mila's notebook to a chaotic pitch. She could barely decipher her count of blood and clean, her temperature charts, numerologies, the excerpts about Tamar and Judah, the *begats* from the Book of Ruth: *Tamar's son Peretz begat Hezron who begat Ram who begat Amminadab who begat Nachshon who begat Salmah who begat Boaz. And Boaz begat Obed who begat Jesse who begat David—*

OF ALL HUMANS DAVID WAS MOST FAVOURED BY THE LORD.

THE DAY BEFORE the departure for Williamsburg, Mila logged into her Book of Days the rise on her temperature chart: 98.6, 98.7.

She was setting the breakfast table when she heard the front door open.

'Hallo, is Josef feeling better?' Zalman called.

Mila stopped setting the table.

Zalman appeared in the doorway. 'Is he feeling better?'

'Josef is not with you?'

'He wasn't well and left synagogue before services were over. He didn't come home?' There was a silence. Zalman adjusted his skullcap. 'Blimela, this is a . . . difficult time for you and Josef. Ten years . . .' Mila did not meet Zalman's eyes, she returned to setting the table. Zalman continued: 'Josef is permitted, expected, to divorce. Blimela, as long as you obey God's commandments, our home is your home.'

Mila bit her lip, hurried out of the room.

In the kitchen, she poured boiling water in the teapot, but she did not bring the tea to Zalman. In her room, she flung herself, face down, on the bed that had once been Atara's and now was Josef's, then she rose, grabbed her handbag, ran out of the apartment.

★

NEW SLOGANS lined the walls.

FAITES L'AMOUR ET RECOMMENCEZ
(make love and make it again)

The sun played on the green shutters and pale pink roughcast of the rue Sainte-Catherine.

RÉVOLUTION, JE T'AIME
(*revolution, I love you*)

On the riverbank, long-haired youths strummed guitars under weeping willows. Bells echoed bells.

LE RÊVE EST RÉALITÉ
(*dream is reality*)

In the Latin Quarter, the statue of the archangel Michael at the Fontaine Saint-Michel wore a red bow tie. Cobblestones lay in mounds. Here, there, a car on its roof, but now the atmosphere was sweet and euphoric. Clusters of people engaged in lively discussion, everyone talking with everyone: workers in blue overalls, girls in mini-skirts, youths in bell-bottoms, and everywhere, as if the city were a book and the walls its pages:

LA RUE DU POSSIBLE
(*street of the possible*)

Mila climbed the five flights to the terrace where she had taken refuge with the students the night of the riot. A frayed note was stuck to the parapet:

MUSE REBELLE, RENDEZ-VOUS À LA PREMIÈRE PLUIE
(*rebel muse, rendezvous at the first rain*)

Mila understood the note was for her, the rebel muse with the Brancusi head.

Had it rained since the night of the riot? She could not remember.

Tomorrow 15:00 hours in front of the Sorbonne. Wear flat shoes...

She headed towards the Sorbonne.

Crossing the rue Champollion, she felt the first raindrops. *The Lord is with me!* She turned back. Heels clattering, she climbed the winding stairs to the terrace. Empty. A burst of heavy drops through sunshine reminded her that it was spring; it must have rained several times since the note was pasted to the parapet; the youth must have come, waited, gone.

She gazed at the gargoyle's mouth pouring into the sky, its glistening eyes. She retrieved the youth's scarf from her handbag, straddled the parapet, tied the scarf around the gargoyle's neck. She stood on the narrow outer ledge of the terrace five storeys above the street. She stroked the gargoyle's elongated snout, stared into its grimacing maw, kissed its wind-eaten lips. 'But David was entirely handsome,' she said. She watched the circling swallows and leaned into their glide. She bent and straightened her knees.

JOSEF REACHED the clinic where he had scheduled his appointment. The Torah verses wept on his shoulder as he entered the tiny tiled cubicle. He placed the velvet pouch that held his prayer shawl and phylacteries outside the cubicle, so the objects of worship would not witness his defilement. He turned off the light and did not look at the magazines with naked women.

The rain pattered on the sill.

As if I were with her, merciful Lord — Is this not the time when she is permitted?

His hands neared his ammah. If God slew him as He slew Onan, death would be welcome, death that would free Mila from her barren marriage.

He was trying with dry hands. *My lawful wife, Mila MilaHeller, dear Lord, a child, a home, a Jewish home, Mila MilaHeller...*

RAIN SPATTERED on the gargoyle's eyeballs. Conceived, conceived, each pattering drop echoed on the narrow ledge ... *Tamar sat near Enayim and Judah thought her to be a harlot, he came in unto her and she conceived, conceived, conceived.*

Would Mila Heller not raise a name for *her* dead?

She held on more firmly to the parapet; straddled it, pulled herself back onto the terrace.

In front of the Sorbonne, the statue of Auguste Comte wore a red necktie. People milled in and out of the large gate. In the courtyard, the statues of Zola and Pasteur brandished red flags. Groups argued next to makeshift stands heaped with manifestos, poems, announcements; *Marx ... Trotsky ... Mao ... Alienation ...*

How would she find the youth Xavier in this crowd?

A large placard read:

IL EST INTERDIT D'INTERDIRE
(*it is prohibited to forbid*)

Mila heard a few notes, then a deep chord. There, in the middle of the courtyard stripped of its cobbles, someone had rolled a baby grand piano. At the keyboard, behind a group arguing passionately . . . she made her way towards him, but he looked down at the keys, face hidden by long curls falling onto a red scarf.

She leaned her back against the piano's bend. The hammers struck the strings. The notes resonated through her. She let herself slide to the ground and under the piano. She was too tall to sit comfortably; she reclined. A fragrance of earth after rain rose around her. Her eyes closed.

The notes climbed up her ankles, along her shins, twirled around her knees, rested on her belly. Her eyes opened. The underside of the piano stretched above her like a black sky trembling with melodies.

She lay her head on a folded elbow.

The notes fluttered in spring exuberance. The pianist's boot pressed the brass pedal, stretched past the pedal, the flat of his jacket brushed the jean-clad thigh. A key chain dangled out of the jacket pocket. At the end of the chain, a lion stood on its hind legs.

The melody crested above her.

The pianist's foot pressed the pedal; the lion advanced, retreated.

The hammers struck a deep chord.

Ten empty years thudded inside her belly.

A few high, scattered notes . . . fading. Silence. Hands

clapped. The wind leafed through the pamphlets on the stands.

'Nem mir,' Mila said.

The youth leaned sideways on the stool, looked under the piano, squinted as if doubting his eyes.

He was not the student of the night of the riots, not Xavier.

She blinked. Their gazes met.

'Nem mir,' she called again.

The student put his hand to his ear, indicating he did not hear or understand.

'Nem mir! Prends-moi! Take me!'

His Adam's apple went up, down. His palm scooped the moulded metal lion on his key chain, and dropped it in his jacket pocket.

She walked quickly; he followed. Her hips swayed up the stairs to the terrace, past tall rectangles of light cast by narrow embrasures. Her hand on her womb, *Quiet now, sleep, hie lee lu lee la . . .* Her hand on the knob, *If it is locked, God is forbidding me.* The door swung open.

JOSEF STOOD in the cubicle, a shakiness in his legs. His breath accelerated. He had presumed this act would be devoid of pleasure without her . . . *Dear Lord, Mila MilaHeller . . .* He was sweating in his thick black coat and the shakiness now was a swaying he had heretofore known as prayer. The release he had called by her name only – inside the cup!

His unsteady hand placed the cup in the metal case that opened on both sides of the wall. The nurse's steps on the vinyl tiles.

He pulled up his black trousers, *Forgive my weakness*. He glued his lips to his fringed garment, *Don't punish me past my strength*.

THE SCARLET SCARF around the gargoyle's neck rippled in the breeze.

Mila bent over the parapet and did not turn to face him.

She lifted her skirt.

Below, the trees had an after-rain sheen.

'Tu es belle,' he said, 'belle et folle.' He enunciated 'folle' as if madness, too, were a form of desire. 'Folle,' he repeated, his tongue rolling over the '*ll*'s' as his arms rounded her waist. He lifted her skirt higher.

She felt the brush of cooler air on her bare skin, between the straps of the garter belt and the top of the seamed stockings.

He unbuckled his belt.

As if it were him, my Anghel . . .

He pulled down her coloured, cotton underwear, her permitted-days underwear. He came in unto her.

She moaned.

'Oui, ma chatte!' he cheered.

And his speaking, too, was a breach, as was the light.

He sank deeper into her.

Her gaze lifted from the glistening canopy to drifting clouds and heavenly gates. *Inscribe a child, O Lord, in the Book of Life.*

She trembled around the hardness inside of her, and her lips opened for the prayer before death: '*Shemah Yisrael Adonaï Elohenu*' (*Hear, O Israel: the Lord is our God*—)

'Oui, mon chaton, Adonaï Echad!' (*Yes, my pussycat, the Lord is One*) the youth exclaimed, laughing, as his seed issued into her.

Book IV

Williamsburg, Brooklyn

MILA WAS IMPATIENT FOR JOSEF'S EMBRACE TO erase the other union and the other seed, even as she prayed for something of that other seed to hold fast.

She packed her suitcase and Josef's in silence; in silence she sat in the taxi to the airport. She would carry the burden; Josef would share the joy.

The youth's impiety still bewildered her. 'I knew these prayers as a kid. Never thought of saying them during — well, this!'

The whole flight home, she wished she could simply ask Josef: Is it better if the seed is Jewish?

Each time she turned to him, he smiled at her.

Josef smiled despite the anguish. If the test established that he was infertile, would Mila resign herself or would she leave him?

Their first night back in Williamsburg, Mila wore the stole that let Josef know she was permitted. Her cheeks were pale, her fist pressed against her breastbone, but the stole, pearl grey and lavender under the lamplight, spun the threads of Josef's desire. He did not notice her

189

clenched white knuckles. He set the pitcher and wash-bowl between the two beds, to wash off sleep's impurity when they woke. By the foot of her bed he swayed, *This month, dear Lord, one child . . .*

The eiderdown rustled as she lifted a corner.

Her open arms: home, his home.

He lay next to her and then he lay on top of her, as prescribed. *Mila, MilaHeller, my pardes, my own garden of paradise* . . . He remembered that they were in the tenth year of their marriage and it set loose in him a desperate energy. In the dark as prescribed. In silence as prescribed.

He did not worry that his passion might be intemperate; she met his thrusts with hers as never before.

He remembered his seed spent in vain and that it was *akin to murder.*

He stilled.

Could he be sensing the other, inside of her? Mila wondered. Her legs circled his hips. Her thighs pulled him deeper in her.

Her heat burned through his anxiety.

He had meant well, Josef reassured himself. He sank deeper.

Her back arched and she let out a cry that startled her even more than it startled him, and Josef wondered, imparadised: *Could this be the sound of my seed, taking root, inside of her?*

Her tears coursed from the back of his hand onto the pillow. He kissed her eyelids, her nose, her lips.

· · ·

Walking to services the next morning, Josef thanked God for creating MilaHeller and for making him the instrument of her cry. She had been so withdrawn during the journey back, last night, her moan . . . *Your ways are unknowable.*

And Josef's steps beat the cadence of her name, *Mila MilaHeller,* and his breath held the imprint of her rapture.

Wanting to be near her, he went home at lunchtime.

She watched his long fingers unfasten the buttons of his black coat.

Seeing her paleness, he said, 'You don't look well. It's been three years since you began—'

'I can't – I won't stop the fertility treatment.'

'Mila, in Paris, I . . .'

'What . . . what in Paris?'

'Nothing, my heart.' He stroked her face. 'Would you be happier if we moved to Paris? It would upset Zalman Stern if we left the Rebbe's court but I'll stand up to him, I'll explain – Would Paris make you happier? I shouldn't have waited so long. Forgive me, forgive—'

'Forgive *you?*'

He kissed her wet lashes. 'I should never have taken you from France.'

'You didn't take me. I wanted to come here, with you.'

THREE WEEKS LATER, the letter from the Paris clinic arrived, informing Josef that he could not conceive. The semen analysis left no doubt; nothing could be done. Mila had been taking the drugs for naught.

Shame flooded him. He would offer to leave her; he must, she so wanted a child.

He placed the thin envelope in a Talmud folio. He looked for the right moment to tell her. 'Mila?' he called from the front door, his voice uncertain, no longer sure she would be there, his home her home, his home a home.

THE TIME of Mila's blood came and she observed that there was no blood.

She wrapped the stole around her shoulders, to let her husband know that she was permitted.

Searching for words to tell her about his infertility, but not finding them, Josef stood at the foot of her bed, silent, and did not go to her.

The next evening, Mila wore the stole again, and again, Josef did not go to her.

'Come to me,' Mila whispered, lifting a corner of her eiderdown.

Mila had never spoken that way, never called him that way; always it was him, at the foot of her bed, waiting for the cotton's soft rustle.

'Josef, I found out – yesterday.'

His slow panic. Had she seen the letter from the Paris clinic? But then why was there joy in her voice?

She took his hand and placed it on her belly. 'I'm pregnant.'

A heat rose in Josef's hand. A wild hope, darting from heart to head, that her cry the night of their return from Paris had been the sound of his seed taking root; God had answered their prayers, miracles happened – but even as the fierce wish tore his chest, he did not step towards her, did not embrace her. She extended an arm.

The stole slid off her shoulder, to the floor, but Josef did not pick it up. Feet rooted to the ground, he wavered between the possibility of a miracle and the letter from Paris, the laboratory report stating that he could never father children.

She pushed away her covers. 'It's me, *Mila Heller*!'

Josef had told Mila that in his thoughts, he still called her *Mila Heller*. Lich-ten-stein sounded so decisive, he had said. Three hammer blows. Whereas Heller – aspirate the *h*, lull the *l*'s, soar with the *r*: *Heller MilaHeller* . . .

'*Lichtenstein*, your name now is Lichtenstein,' he stammered.

'I'm pregnant, Josef!'

His words came out, bewildered: 'I did the test, the forbidden test . . .'

'And I am pregnant!' Her voice was fierce, savage.

At the foot of her bed he swayed, like Zalman by the graves, *God full of compassion* . . . Then his hands joined and he fell to his knees in a fashion Mila did not recognise. Her mouth opened wide. 'Josef?' she whispered.

He scrambled up.

They stood silent; pale and silent.

He stepped away from her, not towards her.

He closed the door to the bathroom. He leaned over the sink. He wept.

★

ANOTHER had brushed her cheek, cupped her breast?

In Paris, of course. An old acquaintance from the lycée, the synagogue? The night she came home without wig or shoes? On what street, what riverbank? The foreign ammah had parted her flesh, parting her from him.

Stoning if she is betrothed.

Strangling if she is married.

Fire if she is a priest's daughter.

Did the Lord punish him because he delighted in her? Rabbi Nachman of Bratslav taught that pleasure in marriage was adultery against the Lord; the pious one feels *pain* during intercourse. Where her name had paced his lips, Josef strained to set His name; instead of *MilaHeller: Kanah, Tsevaot, Shaddaï...*

By day, Josef steered clear of Mila; by night, he cinched the gartel around his loins, the tasselled black sash worn during prayer to separate higher from lower realms, which Josef now wore to bed. What could Josef tender to appease the Lord, except his desire for MilaHeller?

Mila's white sheet, undulating as she turned in her sleep, undid it all. He pulled the sash tighter. He thrust into his dream of her, instead of her.

In the morning, his sore testicles pulled him back into the flesh even as he fastened the first phylactery, winding the black leather strap around his forearm, seven times, even as he fastened the Lord's word to his forehead: *Take care lest the anger of the Lord be lit against you.*

Josef sat on the edge of the couch, head between his hands. Mila entered and sat down at the other end of the couch.

'Don't,' Josef said without looking up. 'Assur.' (*Forbidden*.)

'What, assur?'

'You. To me.'

She rose from the couch. 'How long? How long assur?'

He did not reply. A boy brought up in Williamsburg only would already have gone to the rabbis.

'Forever assur?' she asked. He was silent. 'What you are saying is cruel,' she said.

'What *I* am saying? What the *Law* is saying.'

'What Law?'

'The Law by which we married! *Lo thou art consecrated to me in accordance with the Law of Moses and Israel.*'

'I have always been faithful. Think of it, Josef: Tamar, Ruth . . . the messiah himself will rise from their blood-line. Look at me' – she stared straight into his eyes – 'I was faithful to you and to our Law. I went to Enayim. *Nem mir*, I said. Josef, I'm pregnant. We've waited for this so long. *Pregnant*, Josef!'

His ashen voice. 'I . . . I have to divorce.'

'The only thing missing was a child!'

'A child, this child . . .'

'This child?'

'If it is born . . .'

'*If* it is born!' her voice boomed out of her chest.

He stepped back.

She stepped forward. '*If* it is born!'

He bolted to the front door, stumbled down the five flights.

★

Swish. Mila opened her eyes. Swish swish. Was Zalman sharpening the ritual knives in the kitchen in the middle of the night? Swish. She sat up. She was not in Paris. She rose. She opened the door to the bathroom. Josef's back was streaked. His hand clenched a belt.

He turned and saw her in the doorway, open-mouthed. 'Maimonides instructed rabbinic courts to flog priests not married to virgins—'

'You're not a priest. You did marry a virgin.'

'Are we not believers, Mila? The child . . .'

As he had laboured for words to tell Mila that he was infertile, Josef now laboured for words to tell her that her child might be *forever forbidden to enter the Congregation of the Lord*. He did not find the words. He grabbed his coat; once more he ran down the stairs.

But the Lord had found the words and the Lord watched. At home, the Lord watched whether Josef went near his forbidden wife; in the House of Study, the Lord kept count of Josef's delay, of the hours and days Josef waited before speaking to the rabbis.

If it is proven that the wife committed adultery of her own free will, she becomes prohibited to her husband. The Law allows no mitigation by the husband. Man cannot condone what God forbids. God as well as the husband is offended.

The fear that had knotted Josef's belly, back there, returned. In the penumbra of the House of Study, Josef had come to trust that the word *Jew* need not be a threat; now the House of Study was the threat, the cross's hooked arms that used to whirl on the militiamen's armbands now tore from within.

Josef did not return home for several nights.

★

MILA RETCHED over the sink, rinsed her mouth. Her breasts tingled and she smiled to the unborn child. If it was a girl, she would name her Rachel, in memory of her mother, Rachel Landau; if it was a boy, she would name him Gershon after her father, Gershon Heller—

Josef appeared as out of nowhere. 'Maybe he wasn't Jewish? If he wasn't Jewish then the child – only the child of a Jew – of a Jew and' – beads on his fore head – 'a Jew and a Jewish woman married to another . . .'

'You don't understand, Josef. There are precedents—'

'Such a child . . . the child's status—'

Mila stood up very straight. 'My baby a *status*? Yes, the seed turned out to be Jewish but that was not—'

'Jewish!'

Her eyes widened. 'Is that worse too?'

He fled.

That night, chest-beating, kerchiefed women replaced Mila's long dream of a child, women howling: 'We carried a pure and modest Jewish blood across the generations and Mila Lichtenstein spoiled the blood!' Zalman stood at the pulpit, mouth open but mute. Zalman pursued her with a belt; she ran, missed a step, her cry for help stifled in her throat while streams of prayers that once oriented her rushed past and bounced like spray on rocks.

In the morning, her breasts tingled again. This new life within her, this answer to her pleas, how could it be anything but good?

Her neighbours congratulated her. One brought a potato kugel. 'Spare yourself, Milenka, God has answered your prayers.' Another brought gefilte fish. 'You are carrying a special child, a tzadik.' Zalman added a few words to Hannah's letter, *The Lord has listened to our pleas. Joy with no equal at the news . . .*

Josef left early and came home late. They did not take their meals together, except on the Sabbath. Thursday nights, he still peeled carrots, parsnips and potatoes for the Sabbath chicken soup, but he did so after Mila went to bed. He placed the vegetables in a bowl of water in the refrigerator. Mila's hands trembled when she opened the refrigerator and retrieved the bowl. Her hands trembled as she set down each course on the Sabbath table.

MILA was seven months pregnant when, clearing the Sabbath dishes, she tripped on the rug. Josef lunged and caught her in his arms. He let go of her after she regained her balance, but his hands on her swollen belly felt there was something holy about Mila with child.

After Sabbath was over, Josef rolled up the rug.

From then on, every time Josef came near the Rebbe's house, the curve of Mila's belly blocked the stoop, and Josef retreated.

★

HANNAH CAME from Paris for Mila's lying in. 'Lord in Heaven, what's wrong?' she said when Josef picked her up at the airport.

Later, Hannah asked Mila, 'Is Josef sick? You must tell me. A mother will do anything for her children.'

Mila's hands came to her belly. 'Josef, too, will do anything to save the child.'

'The child needs saving? The Lord have mercy, what do the doctors say?'

'The doctors? No, no, the baby is strong, feel, feel it kicking, tell Josef how you felt it kicking . . . Josef will be home soon, let's set the table.'

Josef did not try to sort through his feelings and obligations during Mila's labour. Sixteen hours, he prayed; sixteen hours he paced the hospital's corridors reciting psalms, uncontrollably, for Mila to be unharmed, until the nurse tapped his shoulder, mother and baby daughter were doing well.

He stood in front of Mila's room in the maternity ward. A nurse carried in the crying infant, and the wails of the forbidden child filled Josef's heart.

'Our treasure is hungry!' Josef heard Hannah say. Then: 'Josef? Is that you at the door? Are you not saying mazel tov to your wife?'

He stepped in.

Mila's shift was unbuttoned. She was pressing a swollen nipple to the tiny mouth. Suckling sounds filled the room. Josef stared at the newborn curled against Mila's bosom, stared at the bared breast, its roundness, its fullness. The new scents of baby oil and mother's milk dizzied him.

'Look at these little fingers!' Hannah cooed. 'Perfect

perfection keneinehoreh (*no evil eye*).' Then: 'When you come to Paris for Passover, you must stay through the summer – why not? Mila will rest. You, Josef, will study with Zalman – what's wrong?'

'A napkin, quick!' Mila cried out as the baby's mouth filled with froth.

Hannah held up the baby to her shoulder and patted the baby's back.

In the empty apartment, Josef watched the overpass as dawn greyed the living-room window. He watched the silhouettes rushing to the first service. The black coats and black hats, the long sidecurls that tamed these men as individuals and had made him feel safe in the streets of Williamsburg, now made them threatening as a group; an army in uniform following one command.

He thought of Mila holding the child to her breast, her face serene at last. He tightened the phylactery's leather strap around his forearm until his fingers tingled. *Forgive me, Lord, let the child drink one year of sweet mother's milk; I will go to the rabbis when she turns one.*

Hannah did not stay the planned three weeks; the couple's deportment unnerved her. She feared her presence might exacerbate that which tore them apart while cleaving them to each other.

In April, the Sterns received a telegram. *We cannot travel to Paris this Passover.* Hannah stared at the empty crib, at the pink blanket she had just finished crocheting. *They must come.*

They did not come. Not this Passover, nor any other.

★

As IF watching over her might cure the infant's status, Josef attended to her faintest cry. It was Josef who caught Rachel's first smile. He was standing by the cradle, calling, 'Rucheleh Rucheleh . . .'

Four-week-old Rachel cooed and smiled back.

It was Mila who caught her first laugh. Eight-week-old Rachel was staring at her own moving hands, staring and giggling.

The nights went by, Mila and Josef in their parallel beds.

Mila sang to the child as her heart sank back and forth with the cradle between the beds: *'Hie lee lu lee la . . .'*

Josef harkened after Rachel's breath as if it were an answer to whether God wanted this child to live.

As Rachel's cheeks filled and rounded, Josef thinned. As she stammered her first words, Josef grew more silent, and his silence was a sin: he was concealing the child's status, he was staying with his wife — but since the night of their return from Paris, Mila and Josef lay in their separate beds every night of the month.

Rachel's first birthday drew near and Josef decided he was too much in his body. Rabbis advised fasting; the less the flesh was gratified, the more one could hope to master it. Josef started to fast Mondays and Thursdays, the days of mourning for the Temples destroyed. But hunger only sharpened his desire, as did the flush of food when he broke his fast after sundown. The sigh of Mila's night shift as it settled on her shoulders, her voice as she lulled the child, *'Hie lee lu lee la ...'* Josef tightened the sash around his waist.

Every night, Mila heard the slump of Talmud tomes on the dining table; every night, Josef lost another battle. There was no clause, no exemption. One night, she heard him cry out: 'Israel cuckolds You and returns but my Mila cannot return to me?'

NOW RACHEL CRAWLED to the front door as soon as she heard Josef's key scratch the lock. She gripped his trouser leg until Josef lifted her in his arms; she seized the brim of his black hat, threw the hat to the floor, burst into bubbly laughter. Josef picked up the hat, placed it back on his head. Again Rachel clasped the black brim and threw it to the floor. Josef pressed to his bosom the little girl with the bow in her hair.

Forgive me Lord, when she turns two I will speak to the Rebbe.

FIFTEEN-MONTH-OLD Rachel was weaned, but Mila did not move the crib from the bedroom; she feared Josef might go back to the living-room couch if the child no longer slept between their two beds.

Mila's blood returned and she resumed her intimate inspections and monthly visits to the ritual bath. Abstaining from the bathhouse was not an option even if Josef never touched her again: little Rachel's marriage prospects would be nil if her mother were suspected of not keeping the laws of family purity. And these laws that had so startled Mila when she first heard them, as an adolescent in Paris, were now the repository of the treasured time when she simply belonged to Josef and Josef belonged to her. Every month, emerging from the small pool of purifying waters, Mila could not help but prepare herself for Josef. Upon her return from the bathhouse, she draped her shoulders in the stole that had let Josef know she was permitted. She stood in front of the three-sided mirror and whispered her name with Josef's intonations, *'Mila MilaHeller ...'* She brought Josef's pillow to her nose and remembered the smell of hay and coarse linen, the smell of the farm boy, back there, but Josef's pillow now smelled of the yellowing Talmud pages his fingers turned, and underneath, the scent of wanting her.

She pulled the stole from her shoulders and folded it in a perfect square. She placed the square in the drawer.

The next day, Josef opened the drawer. His fingers closed on the stole. He brought the soft silk to his nose. *Dear Lord, still my thoughts that they not turn to her; make me stumble and fall, that my hand not reach for her. Dear Lord, do not answer my prayer ...*

RACHEL WAS TWO when Josef began to teach her the aleph-beth.

'א, aleph, *one*, as in: Our Lord is One.

'ב, beth, as in בראשית *(bereshith), In the Beginning ...'* Josef guided the toddler's fingers over the embossed wooden block. 'Why does our Torah begin with the second letter of the aleph-beth and not the first? Feel how the shape of the letter ב is closed to what comes before it? Feel

203

how it opens to what is yet to come? We must not enquire into what comes before the Beginning . . .'

At three, Rachel started nursery school. Every day her dimpled hands danced a puppet rhyme as words gushed through her milk teeth. 'Yuditel and Saraleh and . . .' The snow melted every day in little Rachel's seasons.

'Speak more slowly, we have all afternoon,' Mila coached, but Rachel clutched Josef's legs as more words tumbled from her lips. 'Tatta not all afternoon . . . and Haya push de castle and teacheh say . . .' When Rachel feared Josef's attention might wane, she cried out 'In de beginning! Tory of letters!', and she sat very still until Josef began:

'Story of Letters. All the letters were hidden. God gazed upon the hidden letters and He delighted in them. Then God thought of Creation and each letter came forward and presented its case. Aleph said, "Wouldn't it be fitting to open Creation with the first letter of the aleph-beth?" And God replied, "You, Aleph, I have already chosen to begin my ten commandments." After each letter had spoken, God ruled: "I shall begin Creation with Beth because Beth, *two*, will teach that there are *two* creations: this world and the world to come."'

'Tory of light, Tatta!' Rachel clapped her hands.

And the child's rapture also broke Josef's heart.

When she is four I will go. Surely I will go.

When she is five.

Six.

It will be easier when Hannah visits.

It was not easier when Hannah visited.

At twelve, she will be an adult in the eyes of the Law. I will go before her twelfth birthday.

JOSEF WAS CLIMBING the stoop to the Rebbe's house when twelve-year-old Rachel came running down the block, schoolbag bouncing on her shoulders, hand waving a report card. 'Look, Tatta, look!'

Josef stepped down. This semester, too, Rachel was first in her class. 'Mama will be proud,' Josef said.

'And you, Tatta, are you proud?'

Josef stroked the child's head. 'Of course I am proud.' He lifted the bag from her shoulders. 'What a heavy load for a little girl.'

They headed home, Rachel skipping alongside Josef, Rachel asking over and over in her high singsong, 'You, Tatta, are you proud, are you?'

There is no new sin before she is of marrying age. I will go then, I will not permit the seed to mix.

Twelve-year-old Rachel yearned to be like her peers, seldom in the street without a pram or without holding the hand of a younger brother or sister. At every occasion, she offered to babysit her friends' siblings, and Josef's heart broke as he wondered whether Rachel imagined these were her own children, born happily within the community.

'Your father is strange,' her friends told Rachel, 'he cries when he sees you.' 'All of them cry when they see children, his whole generation,' Rachel replied. 'His crying is different,' Rachel's friends insisted. But Rachel did not perceive Josef's anguish as particular to herself. She attributed the fervour of her father's prayers, his longing and dejection, his heightened concern for her, his silences, to the way people from back there had a darkness in them that they could not escape, a darkness that stemmed from the war against Jews about which they did not speak.

★

SEVENTEEN-YEAR-OLD Rachel came home from school and described the joy that seized her class that morning. Lessons were suspended, tables and benches were piled high against the walls, and all the girls sang and danced, lifting the chair of the first girl to be engaged. 'You should have heard her scream when the chair almost toppled! You know this step, Mama?' Rachel drew her mother into the living room; a true daughter of Israel shies from dancing even in front of her father.

Josef heard mother and daughter tap the new step between couch and coffee table; he heard their laughter, his head bowed.

What am I doing? What have I done?

The telephone rang more often in the Lichtenstein home. Such an accomplished daughter, and good-looking like her mother, tall like her father—

'My Rachel is barely seventeen!' Mila protested.

'You want to wait until all the good boys are taken?'

Josef's old teacher, Halberstamm, heard of Rachel's devotion, of her bright disposition. He, too, called. 'Blessed be the Lord, your daughter has come of age. Let me get to the point, Josef. You know my youngest . . .'

Halberstamm's boy would sit and learn – time was too precious for such a good head to work for a living, but a gifted girl like Rachel would find a job easily, teaching kindergarten or primary school. Later, when work would interfere with child rearing, God would provide.

Rachel Lichtenstein, seventeen, and Shai Yankel Halberstamm, eighteen, met across the dining table. Did Rachel want a husband focused on material pursuits or one who studied Torah? Torah of course. Where did Rachel want to live? Right here, in Williamsburg, close to her mother and father. Would she consider spending a year near his yeshiva after . . .

He meant, after the wedding.

They looked down at the embroidered cloth, they blushed.

At the close of the evening, the two were engaged.

★

JOSEF STARTED to fast every day of the week, not just the days of mourning for the Temple destroyed.

Faced with Josef's anguish, Mila wondered whether *she* should go to a court of rabbinic law to prove her innocence at Enayim, for who knew better than the Lord that Rachel was conceived with His name on her mother's lips? Rachel was as pure as King David, Rachel was beloved by the Lord. A court of law would proclaim Mila's innocence and Josef would eat again, he would stand at the foot of her bed . . .

But judges made mistakes; judges would have burned Tamar and extinguished the line of King David had Judah not proclaimed: *She is more righteous than I.*

Who would come forth to save Rachel if judges erred in this case? Would a court's verdict even matter? Who, in

Williamsburg, would marry Rachel if the slightest doubt hovered over her status? Mila did not go to a court of rabbinic law.

THE REBBE himself danced at the wedding of this bride born of two rescued orphans. In his brocaded white caftan, white socks, laceless black shoes, the Rebbe danced holding one end of his white sash; the bride held the other. His feet traced mystical letter combinations in front of Rachel while she, eyes closed, swayed in prayer: *May Shai Yankel and I form a righteous couple in Israel . . .*

Then it was the father's turn to dance with the bride. Josef nestled Rachel's hands in his. Pitching from foot to foot, he knew this was his last chance to speak before this marriage was consummated, before another seed in Israel was corrupted. But he could hear Rachel's wail as they left the court of rabbinic law: *My marriage invalid? My husband forbidden to me?* He could see Rachel huddled by the low wall outside the marriage hall, clasping her lapel as the men inside danced at other weddings.

The child is innocent! Josef protested.

Of course, the child was innocent. The Torah and the rabbis never claimed that a mamzer's plight was ethical. The Lord commands; man obeys.

The Sages said that those brought to sorrow because they are mamzerim will be seated on thrones of gold, when the messiah comes. Tears coursed down Josef's hollowed cheeks. *Thrones of gold?* Rachel needed her Shai Yankel, she needed her marriage to be valid, she did not need a *throne of gold.*

Some guests already whispered: To sadden a daughter's wedding with such sorrow!

NINE MONTHS after her wedding, Rachel gave birth to a baby girl she named Judith, in memory of Josef's murdered mother, Judith Lichtenstein.

Josef's skin greyed. What degree of self-denial might redeem his silence now?

Rachel named her second child Chaim Yankel in memory of her husband's grandfather deported to Auschwitz.

Josef's nails became brittle.

She named her third child Gershon, in memory of Mila's father.

Her fourth child she named Pearela, in memory of Josef's little sister, and she added the name Alte so this Pearela would live to an old age.

Josef's eyesight weakened. Always he was cold.

When Rachel gave birth to her sixth child, Josef suffered phases of muscle weakness during which he could barely walk. In his hunger-induced trance, he saw his beard swing from the nail in Jesus's palm.

One entry in the Set Table, the authoritative rabbinic code of law, tormented Josef even as it offered some relief about the prospects of Rachel's children:

The husband's declaration of a son's mamzeruth is not believed if the son already has sons of his own for this would taint the son's son of mamzeruth and the Torah has not conferred so wide a power upon a husband.

Now that Rachel had children of her own, a court of law might not be permitted to believe him, if Josef spoke.

The Law would let him evade the Law? Josef wondered. Even if he always knew?

Another entry related how one rabbi went to great length to avoid inflicting the stigma of mamzeruth, allowing for a ten-month gestation in the case of a husband who had been on a journey nine months earlier.

But if judges were no longer permitted to believe him, then Josef would be sentenced like transgressors never brought before a human court — covert desecrators of the Sabbath, masturbators, secret adulterers — he would receive the punishment of kareth, his soul exiled from the Lord's presence. Winter eternal.

And so would Mila.

★

THE WATER BOILED in the blue enamel pot. Mila poured rolled oats into the brisk bubbles, sprinkled a pinch of salt, stirred, lowered the heat.

'Mila?' Josef called.

The wooden spoon stilled. She turned to the warmth in

his voice – as if he had forgotten. 'Oh Josef, can I add fruit to your oats?'

'Not today.'

'But if you don't improve your diet—' The spoon moved again, stirring the film that already wrinkled the oats' surface. The doctor had warned of irreversible cell degeneration; Mila had begged, reminding Josef that not eating was suicide and suicide was forbidden. Still, she had not solicited Zalman Stern or the Rebbe, who might have forced the question of what sin Josef had committed that required such expiation.

'Your eyes – are the drops helping?' she said.

'They are helping.'

Mila saw the bowl of oats, untouched, on the dining table. She leaned against the wall, into the faded wallpaper. She felt so helpless watching Josef's wasting body that she almost wished for a swifter decline. But one block away was the consolation of Rachel living out Mila's dream of a home full of children: boys studying Torah, girls preparing to be mothers in Israel. Rachel's home confirmed that if there had been sin, it was sin for the sake of redemption: *Descent for the sake of ascent.*

And Rachel giving birth to yet another child renewed Mila's resolve to withstand Josef's collapses.

★

WHEN SIXTY-TWO-YEAR-OLD JOSEF grew too weak to walk, Mila helped him out of bed. The first time her hand touched his, they both held their breaths. The square inches of skin against skin awakened their bodies' past joys and their bodies' deprivations, awakened the question of whether the Law might have softened.

The Lord forgiveth the sinner, whispered a voice Josef had heard when he stood next to Florina at mass. But other voices clamoured: *The Lord Himself is offended.*

Mornings, Mila wheeled Josef to the closest prayer quorum. She waited on the stoop if it was warm, by the coat rack in the entry if it was cold. She wheeled him back home after services and helped him into an armchair where he sat, bent over a magnifying glass, scanning the Talmud tomes.

Afternoons, Mila fetched Josef's old eiderdown, the one Florina had once tied with string, which Mila had washed and stowed with lavender sachets, and which she had retrieved one winter day when Josef was especially cold. She swaddled his knobby knees and narrowed ankles, she adjusted the faded tassel closer to his heart.

Tucked in the eiderdown, Josef remembered his two mothers even though he failed to evoke the contours of their faces. He smiled, and Mila, too, broke into a smile as she tiptoed out of the study, leaving the door ajar, slightly, so she would hear if he called.

Evenings, she wheeled him to the prayer quorum, and back to the armchair by the bookcase, where he stayed past the midnight lamentation over the Temples destroyed. Then she helped him into bed. When his breath evened, she closed her eyes.

★

One afternoon, swaddling Josef's feet, Mila whispered, 'Rachel's eldest, Judith . . .'

'Is something wrong with Judith?'

'No, no, nothing wrong. She is . . . seventeen.'

'Judith was born the twenty-first of Kislev 5749 . . . that's right, seventeen.'

'That's what I was trying to say. Judith is . . .'

Dread enveloped him. 'With whom?' he asked, barely audible.

'A good match,' she stammered, 'an honour for our family.'

There was a long silence during which Mila imagined that perhaps Josef did not need to know.

'Who?' Josef whispered.

Some of the pride to which Mila felt she was entitled slipped into her voice. 'Our Judith is engaged to Yoel Stern, Etti's son, Zalman's grandson.'

Josef gasped.

'Judith is so happy,' Mila insisted.

The telephone rang. Mila left the study and Josef heard her accept congratulations from Mrs Halberstamm. His eyes closed. Halberstamm's lineage was passul *(corrupted)* . . . was it now Zalman's turn? Would Rachel and her children corrupt the lineage of all the most pious Hasidim?

No, Judith's engagement to a Stern grandchild was no accident. It was the sign. God was sending Zalman Stern to save them both one last time.

He would go to the Rebbe.

Or perhaps to Zalman himself.

Zalman would cancel the engagement.

Josef thought of his first grandchild, Judith, who as a five-year-old buried her nose in his prayer shawl because she *liked the smell of holiness*. Later Judith stroked the gold letters on Josef's Talmud, declaring that she would become a *woman of valour* and would support her husband's Torah study. She asked whether she looked like her namesake, Josef's mother, and enquired in the community for the walnut-hazelnut roll recipe – not as it was prepared in Kolozvár or Szatmár or Temesvár but the recipe from Maramureş where Grandpa Josef was born. How the girl beamed when Josef remarked that Judith's rolls were the smell of home.

Perhaps not Zalman . . .

Rachel, he should speak to Rachel. Rachel had the strength he never had . . . Rachel would go to the Rebbe, right away she would go.

Let Rachel decide; the children were hers.

He would speak to Rachel.

He would begin . . . come innocent lamb, he would begin . . . like a father who blesses his child . . . *May the Lord permit you to be like the mothers in Israel, like Sarah, Rebecca, Rachel* – three times he would bless her, then he would speak and Rachel, whom they had raised to follow the Lord's command, would go to the Rebbe.

He saw Rachel's children huddled outside the synagogue, pressing themselves against their mother, after he had spoken; he saw Rachel veiling her face in shame. He raised his eyes to the ceiling.

You claim to shun human sacrifice, but it *is* in the name of a father's knife against his son's throat that we ask forgiveness.

His head bowed.

Yes, I will speak to Rachel.

Like Isaac on the altar asking to be bound *tight* to counter his fear of the knife, our Rachel will seek to fulfil the Lord's command, that is how we brought up our Rachel.

In sacrifice, man and God kiss.

Lord God, her neck already bleeding . . .

There is no thicket, no ram? No angel to push the knife aside?

A fly buzzed above him and Josef turned right and left; he could hear the fly but could not see it. He closed his eyes, opened them. He breathed softly, in, out . . . and he could barely see the table in front of him.

Lord God I have heard you. I will speak to Rachel, yes. I will begin: Is it an easy pregnancy you are having? And the children, how are the children? I will tell her . . . before Rachel turns from us, I will tell her that I noticed she started to wear her mother's perfume . . . I will tell her about wild anemones, in Maramureş . . . pleasant fragrances please the Lord, incense was burnt continuously on the Golden Altar.

Yes Lord, I will speak to Rachel.

Josef closed his eyes and saw Rachel take the grandchildren, their lithe bodies and laughter, saw Rachel walk the children to the front door. 'Rachel! Rachel!' he called but Rachel did not look back as she turned the corner and disappeared, forever turned and disappeared. 'Rachel, you must take care of my Mila!' Josef rasped.

Mila rushed in.

'What is it Josef? What should I take care of?'

'Milenka? Ah, it's you. Should we call Rachel back from the country? I am not well, I must see her.' Josef pointed to spines of Talmud folios. 'Please bring me this one . . . and this one . . .' With each volume's thump on the desk, his hollowed frame quivered.

Josef turned the Talmud pages his eyes could read no longer, kept turning them.

When Mila came back into the room, she saw him bent over an upside-down volume. 'You can't see? You can't see at all?'

Josef asked for the set of letter blocks with which he had taught Rachel and then her children the aleph-beth. He tapped the embossed surfaces. He pushed aside blocks until his fingers found what he sought. When his hands lifted, the letters read:

הנני

Hineni, *Here I am, ready* – Abraham's rejoinder to God's: *Take your son . . . whom you love . . . and sacrifice him as a burnt offering.*

'Hineni?' Mila read aloud. She scrambled the letters, feverishly.

Josef's frail neck strained from side to side as the blocks' edges knocked against one an other.

After Mila left the room, Josef tapped the table and arranged the letter blocks again:

הנני

★

MILA STARED at the black-and-white kitchen tiles. Shades drawn, the house was dark and quiet, as empty of children's play as it had been during her barren years. The oppressive heat had allowed Mila to insist that pregnant Rachel and the children stay in the country. Only Judith – who needed to be in the city for a last fitting of her wedding gown – would spend the High Holy Days with her grandparents.

Mila retrieved the Book of Days kept hidden since she came home from the maternity ward with Rachel.

The entries read like an ancient ledger:

עינים (*Enayim*) → *740* → *11* → *2*
פאריז (*Paris*) → *298* → *19* → *10* → *1*
38.5°
Blood 2, 3, 4, 5. Clean 2, 3 ... 5, 7
AND DAVID WAS BELOVED BY THE LORD.

Mila raised her pen. She wrote:

And so is my Rachel, beloved by the Lord for ten generations,
And so is her Judith, pure and white and beloved

Mila drew a garland around *David*. She picked up a second ballpoint pen and coloured each petal of the garland red. The garland sent out shoots that intertwined the names *David, Rachel, Judith* ...

When the doorbell rang and Judith's voice called from the stoop, Mila was so startled her hands gripped the tablecloth as she rose. The carton of milk exploded onto the tiles, the uneaten bowl of oats shattered.

Book V

Manhattan

A MESSENGER DELIVERED THE NOTEBOOK THAT Mila's adolescent hand had labelled so many years ago: *Mila's Book of Days – Private*. Clipped to the cover, a note scrawled on the back of a pharmacy receipt:

Dearest Atara,

I should have come,
but it is too late
to travel back
in time for sundown.
My granddaughter
Judith has read
my notebook.
She will come to you.
Tell her
everything.

—Mila

. . .

Atara had often imagined Mila's knock on the door and a great childhood love returning to her life, but now, *too late to travel back in time,* it was for the knock of Mila's grandchild that Atara waited.

The opening pages of Mila's notebook flooded Atara with memories of the days when Mila commenced a count of blood and clean, and drifted farther from Atara, memories of the Paris dawn in which Atara stood in front of the double porte cochère, a string bag in her hand — a toothbrush, spare underwear — and turned the corner onto the avenue, Paris, the wide world . . .

Atara reached to switch on the lamp by the couch and a postcard fell out of the notebook. On the left of the card: *Mila Lichtenstein* and an address in Williamsburg. On the right, *Atara Stern* but no address. The card was dated 1958, the year Atara left.

It had taken ten years until, in the euphoria of spring 1968, Atara sent Mila her address and phone number. From then on, with each subsequent move, Atara had sent a postcard: New York, Cambridge, Los Angeles, New York, San Francisco, New York . . . With each unanswered card, Atara reminded herself that she knew before leaving that she would lose her family, she knew that Mila could not open her door to a renegade sister without jeopardising her children's marriage prospects. Mila would get in touch once her children were raised and married.

The time for marrying children passed.

Atara tucked Mila's unsent postcard in the back of the notebook and discovered an airmail envelope, from Paris. One typed paragraph informed Monsieur Lichtenstein that he could not conceive.

Evening fell in the loft as Atara read and reread Mila's notebook, trying to make sense of the numerology, the biblical fragments, the laboratory letter. As the story came together, her eyes blurred with tears.

She rose and stared out the window.

Why would the girl come to her? It seemed to Atara that long ago a deal was struck: Atara won her freedom but lost existence in her family. Was the deal being renegotiated after forty-seven years? Her heart began to race.

Williamsburg, Brooklyn

IN THE WOMEN'S BALCONY OVERLOOKING THE prayer hall, Judith pressed her forehead against the lattice. *I am – I am and my children are –* she could not bring herself to finish the thought.

In the hall below, her brothers danced with the Bridegroom of the Law, they danced unaware that they were misbegotten. In step with her brothers, shoulders already stooped from so much study, her Yoel. The invitations had been mailed, *Judith and Yoel, ceremony at half past six—*

Before the women could see her tears, Judith wound her way to the back of the balcony, down the crowded stairs, through the maze of prams filling the street and pavements.

Just two Sabbaths ago, she had strolled down these blocks almost singing aloud: *How goodly are your tents, Jacob!* How goodly in the soft gleam of a lit prayer hall, how goodly the hushed land of Williamsburg when traffic halted to celebrate a Holy Day. Two Sabbaths ago, Judith knew that she, too, would wear a white kerchief and lean over a stroller while her husband danced the seven rounds; she, too, would bring into this world souls waiting to be born, and when all the souls had come down and the messiah arrived—

But did souls like hers hasten the coming of the messiah, or delay it? Every night since reading her grandmother's notebook, she had researched seed issuing as unpious books said it would, as her father's books said it must not.

She headed north, towards the Williamsburg Bridge. She would keep the promise she made to her grandmother: Before bringing the secret to the rabbis, she would see the one who left, May Her Name Be Erased.

She climbed the pedestrian ramp. She had crossed the bridge before, but never in the dark, alone. Four youths leaned against the orange fence, watching her approach – she should have tucked the string of pearls under her collar, she must not run, they would outrun her. *HaShem, do not abandon me.*

Once she had passed the youths, her fingers hooked the necklace. Would she be asked to return the pearls, her betrothal gift from Yoel, when the secret was known? Shame burned her cheeks and spread to her neck.

A rumble approached from behind; a slap of rectangular light; the train rattled and teetered off, pulling its shadow after it.

A fenced footbridge crossed over the tracks. She pressed her face against the fence. Amidst the roar of a honking truck, of another passing train, her lips sounded out the verdict of her father's books: *'I am forbidden.'* Her throat tightened. She swayed behind the fence as if the footbridge were the women's gallery and the track below were the Rebbe's dais; in her prim suit, heeled pumps, she swayed as if the entire world were a prayer hall and the night above were the Lord's veiled eye; and her body bowed with the fear that the Lord no longer looked upon her with compassion, that the Lord had abandoned her even before she was born.

The clang of a train interrupted her swaying. A luminous J inside a circle trembled on the rear of the last carriage, and shrank. A tall lamp-post lit the track. She wanted to curl around the post and rest. She set out again.

On the edge of Manhattan was a brightly lit field where youths her age aimed balls at rings. Some tossed the ball inside the ring even as they ran, even as others jumped in front of them. She stared at the light-footed humans playing in the night, then walked on.

Office towers were lit but nothing moved inside. An eerie glow hovered over the city. There lived Atara Stern.

Manhattan

ATARA PREPARED FOR JUDITH'S ARRIVAL. SHE covered the human representations, the oil paintings in which Judith would see only transgression: a grandfather gazing inquisitively from his carved armchair, found in a Prague street market; a Roman grandmother in luxuriant pink, lavender and violet; an unfinished sister with a gauzy ribbon in her hair, from a collector she knew in Strasbourg. She left uncovered the medieval maps and walled gardens.

She paused in front of ink-jet printouts tacked to a white foam-core board. A few years earlier, when smoke and ash had covered lower Manhattan, her producer had e-mailed a link to a video of a stoning. She had printed a few stills: an oblong blue ball stuck in the ground; a blue veiled form struggling out of the ground – human, hands bound, female; a circle of bearded men around the writhing red pulp. What could she *do*?

In the retreating light, the blood seemed to spread from the stills to the mounting board, to the philosophy books, the novels, poems, to the labelled canisters of her films . . . She turned the board so the printouts would face the wall.

She put on a long-sleeved dress, set two paper cups on a paper napkin – but there was no concealing that she was Atara Stern, the one who left, the daughter Zalman mourned. The stories about her surely frightened the girl. Who was Atara Stern in those stories? A traitor? Dead? Worse: a questioning Spinoza? Ah, of course, no story at all: *May Her Name Be Erased.*

But she would help the girl even if the girl did not want to be helped; Mila knew to whom she was sending her granddaughter and could not expect otherwise. She would help even if old Hannah and Zalman had to hear about their lost daughter enticing a young girl to leave. The ancient laws had done enough damage.

Atara checked the landing. No one.

The phone rang. A number in Brooklyn. Silence on the line, then a sharp breath that Atara still recognised. 'Mila?'

There was no reply, but it was Mila – Mila not wanting to compound, by talking, the sin of dialling on a Holy Day.

'She isn't here yet,' Atara said.

Another sharp breath. Atara heard Mila pray that Judith, daughter of Rachel, cross the bridge safely, then Mila's breath became a whisper: 'She won't ring a bell on Simchath Torah.'

'I'm sitting where I will hear every step in the stairwell.'

'She swore that she would go to you.'

'She swore? Then it wasn't *her* decision?'

'No.'

'What do you want me to do?'

'Of course I want her here, with us, in Williamsburg.'

Remembering how Mila would attach her most intense hopes to the least likely outcome, Atara said, 'But if she won't keep the secret? If she believes her fate and the fate of her siblings, her mother, is to live disgraced on the fringe of the community?'

'I . . . I can't let her destroy the family.'

'So in that case you would want me to help her, to help her leave?'

'She's a good girl. Perhaps you can help her understand I was faithful . . . always faithful.'

Atara realised Mila was not seeking to provide Judith with a way out but rather with a trapdoor back in.

'How much time do I have with her? When is her wed—' The stairs creaked. 'She's here,' Atara whispered and rushed to open the door.

Atara expected a Hasidic girl from Williamsburg to stand timidly in the entrance, but Judith burst past her into the room, arms crossed, face flushed.

'What is it my grandmother wants you to tell me?'

She seemed far too young to be engaged. So late at night, she ought to be tucked into bed and told a fairy tale.

Judith strode across the loft and stopped in front of the window. Her back was stiff. She was afraid Atara's walls, chairs, afraid the books piled high on every surface, the film canisters, might contaminate her.

'You must be Judith,' Atara said. 'I'm glad you came. You walked all the way, of course. Let me take your coat.'

Judith whirled around. Wrists crossed on her chest, she hugged the lapels of the dark jacket she wore over a straight skirt that ended, as prescribed, four inches below the knees. She was taller than Mila, but she had Mila's plum-blue eyes and dark hair. She was as beautiful as Mila was back then.

'What did you do to my grandmother?'

Atara's hand came to rest on Mila's notebook. 'If only I *had* done something.'

Judith turned her gaze away. 'I don't need you to tell me that out here everything is permitted.'

'I'm hardly one to speak of what is forbidden or permitted. I think your grandmother would like you to . . . understand what happened.'

'I know what I am. What my children will be. And their children.'

The girl's tone was defiant but Atara could detect recent tears. She pointed to a chair across the table, she poured water in the paper cups. 'Sit, Judith, sit.'

When Judith at last sat down, Atara saw that she had not hung up the phone. She said, to what she realised might be an audience of two, 'If, when this story is over . . . if you return to your grandmother, Mila . . . please tell her that I . . . tell her – ah, let us begin, let us begin with Zalman Stern when he was your age, seventeen . . .'

Atara told the story of Zalman in Transylvania, of Josef and his sister Pearela, of Florina and her son Anghel; she told of pious Mila at the seminary, and the wedding of Josef and Mila; she told what she could about the ten barren years of marriage.

★

JUDITH'S HEAD was inclined, her nape exposed. For hours, she had listened without stirring. Atara had encouraged her to talk, to react, to share what she knew, but the girl had been silent. Atara pulled back the curtain that screened the sleeping alcove.

'It's almost dawn. You need rest. We'll start again when you wake.'

The girl curled up on top of the coverlet and fell asleep within seconds. Her eyelids quivered, her breath softened, her mouth half parted.

Atara felt a hint of the want that had seized Mila all those years ago, the want for a child that Atara herself had not heeded.

A truck barrelled down Canal Street.

Judith moaned. Her arm lifted, came to rest above her head, then she was still again.

Atara lay down on the couch.

While none of Atara's films had been about the Hasidic world, she had often imagined that in the front row of her audience sat an adolescent on the threshold, choosing between staying in and setting out . . .

It was clear that Judith had never imagined herself outside, dead to her parents as Atara was dead to Zalman and Hannah.

It had been hard enough for Atara who had *wanted* to leave, who had felt exhilaration in risking everything.

When she had learned that Zalman hired a detective to bring her home, Atara spent the money she had saved on a ticket to the United States where she would be considered an adult at eighteen. Atara thought of the nights in Manhattan train stations. The club slapped against the policeman's hands as he commanded slumped men to 'Move, move on!' A mumbling woman emerged from a sea of shopping bags. Eighteen-year-old Atara lifted her backpack; she, too, circled the station.

Atara could spare Judith the struggle for food and shelter, she could even put her through college, but she could not spare her the losses, could not spare her the anguish of shaping a new self.

She would need time with the girl, much more time than this one night, and the girl would need time for solitude. She would take Judith to the country, Mila would find a way to arrange it, to explain the girl's absence. Perhaps she would show Judith her first film, about a girl standing on escalators, in front of ticket counters . . . She would call a psychiatrist the next day, ask for advice, she would request an appointment for Judith, she would try to be there for the girl in all the ways that no one had been there for her . . . and if one day Judith wanted to become a presence in Atara's life . . . how lovely it might be, for each, to have another who understood where she came from and the distance travelled. Pulling up the chenille throw to her chin, Atara let herself imagine an ending in which she rocked the girl in her arms and whispered in her ear, 'It's over, you're here, in Manhattan, the sun is rising, let's fill the kettle with water . . .'

When Atara opened her eyes, Judith was praying, turned to the morning sun.

Atara rose quietly.

After Judith had finished her prayers, Atara rinsed some grapes and placed them on a paper plate.

'Thank you, but I'm not hungry,' Judith said.

'Look, a *paper* plate and the grapes haven't come in contact with any of my utensils. You can eat. You must eat.'

Judith tore a grape, held it between index finger and thumb, hesitated as if she wondered whether she must now say a different blessing. At last, her lips moved and then she brought the grape to her mouth, swallowed, and urged Atara to continue with the story.

'But it is *you* who were there, Judith. You tell me what happened. It will be good for you to speak.'

'Nothing forbidden will be good for me.'

'You came back from the country, you arrived at your grandparents'. What happened?'

Judith was silent.

'It is terrible to feel one has no one to talk to,' Atara said.

Judith had expected Atara's place to be loud and decadent, but the high-ceilinged loft was quiet, contemplative, and made her think of her father's study except that the light here was softer, islands of light, not the bare ceiling bulbs of her parents' home. She had expected a fallen Atara Stern, unbefitting makeup, tawdry clothes . . . Atara's dress would be considered immodest in Williamsburg, but it was not unseemly and the silver-white hair Atara Stern should be ashamed to expose framed a lined face that smiled . . . smiled at Judith even though Atara knew how Judith's mother was conceived, smiled as if it did not matter, not at all . . . and Judith wanted to curl up in Atara's arms, curl up and cry, it was not what she had imagined about one who left, May Her Name—

'I tried to be good, I would have deserved to marry Yoel Stern,' Judith whispered.

Atara nodded.

Judith continued: 'It's true I have no one to talk to . . .

and who am I if Grandpa Josef is not my grandfather? There's nothing to figure out because nothing can change what is spelled out in the Torah . . . nothing . . . I feel lost, lost— When I was a little girl, our kindergarten teacher asked what everyone wanted to be when we grew up. One girl cried out, "A fireman! With a red truck!" The teacher scowled, the right answer was *not*, definitely *not* "fireman". She turned to me. "Judith, what do *you* want to be?" I didn't know the right answer . . . "A mother?" I asked. The teacher kissed me, she smiled, other little girls yelled, "A mother, I want to be a mother!" So I did know . . . then . . . but now . . .'

Judith's smooth, white throat pulsed as she swallowed.

'What happened when you came back from the country?' Atara asked.

Judith put a hand over her mouth as if to keep from speaking.

Atara waited.

Judith started haltingly. 'I ran into my Yoel in front of Heimishe Bakery, on Lee. We didn't stop to speak — es past nicht (*it is not proper*) — but he . . . I . . . we smiled, we couldn't help it, our paths crossed, I clutched my shopping bag as if Yoel could see the tiara and wedding veil inside. I waited at the corner until I stopped blushing, and turned onto Clymer, but Grandma Mila was not waving at the bow window even though Mummy had discussed everything, which bus line, which stop, at a quarter to five — I rang the doorbell. No one answered. The curtain was drawn in Grandpa Josef's study — a meheireh refiheh sheleimeh far mein (*a speedy and complete recovery for my*) Zeidi Josef, Amen — the curtain was drawn but Grandpa likes the feel of light even if he doesn't see it any more. "Baabi? Zeidi?" Everything so still. I went around the corner, down the alley, to the back of the house. "Baabi? Zeidi?" There, too, everything was still. *Is Zeidi dead, God forbid?* I hurried to the front of the house, up the stoop, I turned the knob. The door opened. Grandma Mila's prayer book lay open on top of the secretaire — something was wrong. I kissed the page, closed the book, kissed the cover. The dining room was tidy and empty. I followed the smell of medicine to the door of the study — something stirred in the kitchen, Gottenyu (*dear God*), Grandma Mila was slumped on the tiles in the middle of broken dishes and a spilled carton of milk. I dashed to help her up but Baabi drew her knees to her chest, her wig was askew, it was like I needed to remind her, "It's *me*, Judith!" Her skirt, HaShem yerachem (*the Lord have mercy*), it wasn't modest on her thighs. "Baabi, do you hear me?" She clasped my forearm, with her other hand she pushed against the floor and lifted herself up. A notebook fell from her lap into the spilled milk. I leaned to pick it up but Baabi shook my arm until I dropped it. The notebook fell back into the spilled milk. "Is it Rachel?" Grandpa Josef's voice so faint behind the closed door of the study. Grandma Mila's finger came to her lips. "Shh, let's not tell him you're here, he needs rest", and she hurried down the corridor. A drop of milk widened on the page, blurring a word, the word below — I couldn't help it, I picked up the notebook, placed it on the counter, dabbed the wet pages with a paper towel, placed the salt and pepper shakers on the notebook's corners so it would stay open and dry faster. I put down the shopping bag with my tiara and veil, I picked up the broken china, mopped the milk. The house was so quiet. It was the first time I was at Zeidi and Baabi's without a younger brother or sister. A page of the notebook puckered up, I pulled it flat. In

Grandma's handwriting: *Next month, dear Lord, let it be me. Give me a child or I will die*—

'Grandma Mila slapped the notebook shut. I was ashamed, I ran upstairs. Grandma Mila soon came after me, she hugged me, she said a kaleh meidel must not be sad, it was not good for the complexion, I had done nothing wrong, how could it be wrong to pick up a notebook and dry its pages? She rocked me, I laughed, I asked if she and Zeidi wanted to see how the veil and tiara fitted. "It's late, my heart," she said, "Zeidi is resting. You'll show him tomorrow, when you try on the dress, the seamstress is coming at nine." We went down to the kitchen to prepare dinner. The notebook was no longer on the counter. I asked, "Is the notebook about how Zeidi Josef and you survived?" Sometimes people from back there don't want to talk about it but Grandma said, "Yes, how we survived and decided to live." I knew about Grandma Mila and her parents rising in the middle of the night in the synagogue where they were locked up, how the others who stayed behind recited the prayer for those who leave, I knew that Grandma Mila, as a little girl, had crossed the Nadăş River on her father's shoulders—

'"Are they teaching it to you in school," Grandma asked, "are they teaching you about the Rebbe's escape?"

'"Of course, in kindergarten. How God sent a dream to a man who could save Jews: *You must rescue the Rabbi of Szatmár or your venture will not succeed.*"

'Grandma Mila stared up at the ceiling. "Ah, the dream . . ." Then her head snapped forward and she said, "You do understand that the Rebbe himself, may his merit protect us, wanted to get on that train. You understand that he abandoned his community and his

Hasidim", and she said apikorsus (*heresy*) about how the Rebbe escaped from Transylvania with the help of a Zionist – God forbid, no one but HaShem saved our Rebbe!

'Grandma Mila explained that sometimes the only way to bring more holiness into the world is to shroud an act in sin, so that Satan will not notice its goodness and interfere, and I knew this from school but it is never something we decide to do, only God and his angels.'

There was a silence. Judith started again.

'Then Grandma Mila said, "My Josef is preparing himself for the next world, he fears for his soul." We both started to cry because Grandpa Josef – if the messiah doesn't come before the Lord calls back his soul – Grandpa Josef has nothing to fear, he will go straight to the Garden of Eden and I said Mummy wants to be here, she wants to come back right away if Grandpa Josef's health, God forbid—

'"In her state? Your mother must not come back, must not. She would busy herself with wedding preparations, in the eighth month it isn't safe. Your mother will come back from the country for your wedding, after Simchath Torah. Don't worry, mein kint, your Zeidi will live to a hundred and twenty years. You're not eating? My own grandchild goes hungry in my house? Eat, child, eat. You finished? Say your blessing and go to sleep, a young body needs lots of sleep."

'I woke in the middle of the night. I saw a ray of light under the door. I rose. The lamp on Grandma's night table was lit but Grandma's bed was empty. The house was so quiet. I tiptoed down the stairs. Grandma Mila was sitting at the kitchen table, in front of the notebook. She was crying. "Is Zeidi Josef very sick?" I asked. She looked up, closed the notebook, stared at the dried flower under the cellophane dust jacket. "*Anémone des bois*," she said and she said Grandpa Josef loved the fragrance of this flower, it reminded him of spring, back there, it reminded him of Maramureş and did I know that in Maramureş, where Grandpa Josef was born, where Florina used to keep an eye on little Josef, in his first mother's orchard . . . did I know that in spring, in Maramureş, the meadows were yellow and white with daisies . . . then, as if just noticing I was standing in the doorway: "You're up? You want dark circles under your eyes on your wedding day? Go to bed."

'I went back up. I heard the door of the study open and close and I thought of the love between Grandpa Josef and Grandma Mila and I prayed that such a love would bind my Yoel to me – but with many more children, if it pleases HaShem.

'The seamstress arrived at nine for the last fitting of my wedding gown. She fastened the tiny satin buttons of the bodice and Grandma Mila said, "Seventeen, one for each of your seventeen years." When I turned around, the seamstress put a hand over her heart and said I looked just like Grandma Mila looked when she was young – I wasn't sure how to feel because everyone always said Grandma Mila had been the most beautiful woman in Williamsburg.

'I asked if I could show the wedding gown to Grandpa Josef.

'Grandma Mila said no.

'After the seamstress left, Grandma went into the study and I heard Grandpa Josef ask, in a voice so weak, whether Rachel had arrived. Grandma said no. Then Grandpa Josef asked whether Zalman Stern had arrived for the wedding and Grandma again said no but it wasn't true because Zalman Stern *had* arrived from Paris and everyone *knew* he was staying with his son Schlomo, everyone knew Zalman Stern had come from Paris to officiate at the wedding of his grandson Yoel with Judith Halberstamm, the granddaughter of the two orphans Zalman had rescued.

'"Zalman Stern isn't here yet," Grandma Mila repeated.

'The spoon tinkled against the medicine bottle, the pillows puffed . . . I was afraid all alone with Grandpa so sick and Grandma Mila not telling the truth.

'When she came out at last, I said that if Zeidi, God forbid, was very sick, I *must* call Mummy right away.

'"I told you, my heart, your mother mustn't come. The shock . . . it might—"

'"Is something wrong with Mummy?"

'"Is that Rachel I hear?" Grandpa called.

'Grandma ran to the study.

'I didn't understand why Grandma Mila was treating me like a child with my wedding in three weeks and my bride-class teacher just taught how even we believers are conceived in this lowly manner, how a man and a woman . . . the Lord's ways are unknowable – if something was wrong with Mummy, with her health, God forbid, I, the eldest daughter, ought to know and what if Mummy had Grandpa Josef's sickness – how could I help if I didn't know? The notebook? Did the notebook explain Grandpa's illness and why Grandma Mila was acting so strange?'

Judith started to pace inside the loft, back and forth she paced as if trying to flee who she had become since reading the notebook, as if trying to hold back an earlier self. When she spoke again, her voice was hoarse. She stopped, startled by the low, deep pitch that could not be hers; she started again.

'I reached into the kitchen cabinet, on the highest shelf. The notebook opened to the last page of writing. I stared at the red garland; the words stared back at me, stronger. The red petals twisted around *King David . . . Rachel . . . Judith . . .*

'I knew which pages were important, the ones smudged by tears.

'There were French, Hungarian, Romanian words . . .

'There was an envelope addressed to *Monsieur Lichtenstein*, from Paris.

'One paragraph and numbers: *Nous regrettons de vous informer . . .*

'In the notebook, the same passage, over and over. Over and over.' The words stumbled like rocks out of the girl's throat: '*Tamar sat near the entrance to Enayim and Judah thought her to be a harlot and he came in unto her and she conceived.*

'I knew it was terrible but I didn't know what it meant. I rushed out of the house – under the elevated track, on Broadway and Marcy. The rumble of a Manhattan-bound train – whom could I ask? Not Tatta, not my teachers – which books could I look up, girls don't study Mishnah or Gemarah, also not the Shulchan Aruch, I crossed into north Williamsburg with the artists, into the library on Division. The woman told me I wanted the *Encyclopedia Judaica* and I had to go to the Grand Army Plaza branch or to the Borough Park Branch . . .'

Judith swayed back and forth.

'*Marriage between forbidden people is void, not valid.* Let the messiah come, please let the Temple be rebuilt,

I walked back to our Williamsburg. Was Mummy's marriage void? I went around the block, once, twice, one does not run from God's trials Mummy would say, Mummy would go to the Rebbe — will Tatta be encouraged to remarry and have new children, *legitimate Jews,* while I, my brothers, sisters . . . the ten mamzerim of Williamsburg — "Judith!" Running towards me, Grandma Mila in her housedress and slippers. She pulled me up the stoop, inside the house, into the kitchen, she closed the door, ran to her *T'nach,* the *T'nach* trembled in her hand, it opened to the story of Tamar and Judah. She pointed to a verse. "*Zodequa mimeni.* See? *More righteous than I,* that is what Judah said about Tamar — you *will* be happy, you *must* be happy, that is why Josef sacrificed all the happiness in his life — think, think carefully before you decide to go to a rabbi, think about whether you want to undo the silence for which my Josef sacrificed the happiness in our marriage, what seems right to you now may begin to haunt you, if you don't want to spare yourself, spare my Josef," and she asked if I knew about Florina — of course I knew. She said she heard Florina call across the bluff: "*Anghel! Anghel!*" She said Florina's voice was the voice of a mother calling for her son, she said Josef yearned for his second lost mother separated from her not by war nor death but by *us, us.* She said, "I did not understand the silence that would save my daughter would further cripple him," then she made me swear I would go and see Atara Stern so that I would know — know what?'

Judith looked into Atara's eyes, fiercely. 'Atara Stern will save me when God cannot?'

'You need time, and a quiet space, inside of you. Stay with me, Judith, even if only a few days. We can go to the country, tonight, after sundown. We'll bring food with all the right certifications, everything kosher to *your* standards. You need to rest, to think—'

'Think about what? HaShem created us to keep his commandments, what should I think about?'

'You need to look into this further—'

'I looked into it. I searched my father's books, I saw: *God will reward the repenting adulteress and her reward is that her offspring will die young, young enough so her sin will not enter the congregation.*'

'Where did you read such a thing?'

'I read that one posek (*jurist*) advises that the word *mamzer* be tattooed, by a non-Jew, on the baby's forehead – to make sure a mamzer will not marry into the congregation.'

Atara placed her arm around the girl's shoulder. 'Judith there are other worlds, where marriage is not so much about lineage, where parents can love their children unconditionally—'

Judith clamped her hands over her ears. 'I don't want to hear apikorsus.'

'I'm putting a set of keys in your jacket pocket. Stay with me, Judith.'

'My nisoyon (*trial*) is to get closer to HaShem, not to those who abandon Him.'

'You need time—'

Judith strode across the loft. 'I don't need *time*, I need the opposite' – she stopped in front of the oven clock – 'eight thirty?' She rushed to the coat rack. 'Grandpa Josef is waiting.'

'So you did see Josef?'

'Not yet. I told Grandma Mila that I would go to you in Manhattan if I could see Zeidi in the morning and take him to synagogue.'

'Josef is well enough to go to synagogue?'

'He wants to hear Zalman Stern lead services.' Judith slid her thin arms into the sleeves of her jacket and walked to the front door.

Atara grabbed a scarf and rushed after her.

Judith headed east, towards Williamsburg. She walked oblivious to traffic. Atara held Judith's elbow with one hand, with the other she pushed stray wisps of hair under the scarf.

They started across the bridge. Cars whizzed by. A train clanked as it started and stopped. During a lull in the din, Atara asked whether Judith had thought about her fiancé, about what Yoel would want her to do.

'Yoel would want what HaShem wants,' Judith replied.

The horn of a tugboat sounded on the river below.

'But there are indications that this . . . *status* no longer applies since your Grandpa Josef kept quiet so long,' Atara said.

'My mother's name should have been on the register the rabbis keep, the register of people forbidden to marry in our community.'

'But if the Law says it's too late now – certainly *you* believe the Law must be obeyed. We'll check the Law—'

'*We* will check? *We* will decide? A court of Law must decide.'

'There are places – Jewish places – where you could study the Law yourself—'

'I told you, I read my father's books.' Judith clutched the orange fence. She looked for the river but car lanes, tracks, guardrails blocked the view of the water, nothing seemed to link Williamsburg to Manhattan. 'At a mamzer's circumcision we must skip the prayer *Kayem at hayeled hazeh* (*Preserve this child*). The Shulchan Aruch says: *Ein mevakshim alav rachamim* (*We do not ask mercy for him*). We do not ask that this child live.'

'Judith! That can't be what was meant.'

Judith turned around and took hold of Atara's hand. 'I know you want to help, I can see you're not a bad person, you're only mistaken.' Judith patted Atara's hand like a parent consoling a child, then she let go and set out towards Williamsburg.

Atara tried to keep up with the girl. With every step Judith took, the closeness that had seemed possible in the loft, that still seemed possible just seconds ago, was slipping away. Atara scurried after Judith still hoping she might whisk her to some place and time where the girl would smell the earth after rain, and hear the birds sing again, a place where Judith could watch the world renew itself.

Judith's lips moved to the rhythm of her hurried steps: 'I am forbidden. So are my children and my children's children, forbidden for ten generations, male or female. I am . . .'

Judith's lips were still moving when she came down the pedestrian ramp. Before reaching the pavement, she stopped and pulled the seams of her thick stockings, to straighten them.

★

A SHADOW peeled away from the wall. The coat, too heavy for the season, floated around the shoulders. The coarse, synthetic hair accentuated the pallor of the face.

'Mila?' Atara whispered.

Mila's gaze travelled from Atara to Judith, searching for signs that a solution had been found.

Judith climbed the stoop and entered the house.

Mila and Atara hugged. Their bodies recognised that they once shared the same bed and the child in each held the other tight.

Nesting her chin on Atara's shoulder, Mila wiped her tears. 'How is she? What has she decided?'

Atara stroked Mila's shoulder and wiped her own tears. 'She needs time.'

'Her wedding is next week.' Mila nodded to passing neighbours on their way to synagogue. Her hand came to Atara's forehead and tucked a strand of hair back under the scarf, then pulled up the collar of Atara's dress. Smiling a poor stab of a smile, Mila whispered, 'Can I get you a shawl? I think I have something that would match your dress.'

Judith appeared in the doorway. 'Zeidi isn't in his study?'

'Yuditka, your Zeidi Josef is in shul. He wanted to go early so he could be wheeled to the front before the crowd arrived. I brought him then I rushed back, to be here if – when you returned. Let's go in, let's have breakfast.'

Judith's lower lip trembled. She hesitated and started down the stoop.

Mila extended a hand. 'Stay with us, Yuditel, stay here with us a while. Wait! Wait for us! Let's all go to shul together.'

Judith stepped away from her grandmother, so it was

Atara who threaded one wrist through Judith's elbow, the other through Mila's, and they walked together as if they belonged to one family, one life, they walked a few blocks towards the celebration of the Festival of the Law and Mila let herself hope that the men's rounds would still dance Judith to the wedding canopy.

Atara planned to explain to Mila that the first step towards a decision was for Judith to learn to think for herself, that it might be good for Judith to get away from Williamsburg, even if only for a few days. Mila would find a way to arrange it. Perhaps the girl would come to Atara's loft this very evening and they would leave together for her cottage in the country.

Atara whispered to the girl that she would wait for her, she reminded Judith of the key in the pocket of her jacket.

Mila, Atara, Judith entered the street filled with strollers and clusters of mothers. Atara's attention drifted to the realisation that she might soon see her father. Her heart pounded. She would pull aside a young boy after services, she would instruct the boy to tell Zalman his daughter, Atara, was in the women's balcony and wanted to wish him a Good Holiday. Perhaps Zalman would call for her, perhaps Zalman would agree to see the daughter he declared dead, and they would meet, she would kiss her father's hand as after a long journey . . .

When Atara had felt secure enough in her new life, after her first film, Atara sent her number to Hannah. In the middle of the night, the telephone rang. In the receiver, Zalman was asking, commanding, that Atara repent and return to *our Hasidic home*. The word *home* set Atara sobbing, but when she failed to reply that she was coming back, Zalman cursed her, called her a *zonah*

– a harlot. Atara placed a finger on the switch. Click. The line went dead for thirty-seven years.

There had been times when Atara had considered appearing on her parents' doorstep, times when she needed to believe her parents would be happy to see her even if they suspected she might not keep the Sabbath – she would lie if they asked, if it made it easier for them – there had been times when Atara needed to believe that her parents longed to hear her voice as she longed to hear theirs, but when Atara reached out to her younger siblings, they warned: Your father's heart might give – have you not done enough damage?

The thought that within minutes she would see her father draped in his prayer shawl, the thought of Zalman's singing voice reaching Judith's torn heart caused Atara to squeeze Judith's and Mila's elbows as they approached the synagogue. Mila, Atara, Judith were about to enter when a very pregnant woman stepped in front of them.

'Is zie a Yid?' the woman asked. (*Is she a Jew?*)

'Ver?' Mila replied. (*Who?*)

The woman glanced at Atara.

'Avadeh!' Mila said. (*Of course!*)

'Sie zeht nicht os vie a yid.' (*She doesn't look like a Jew.*)

'Ober avadeh ist zie a yid.' (*But of course she is a Jew.*)

'Und voos ez mit ihr levish und mit irh tiechel? Zie is nicht tzniesdik. Zie can nich arein gein.' (*What about her dress and her kerchief? She is not dressed modestly. She cannot go in.*)

Atara looked down at her hem. Was she only imagining that the dress covered her knees?

The pregnant woman stared at Atara's neckline.

Atara's hand came to her collarbone – at least half an inch was exposed. She should have accepted Mila's offer and taken the shawl.

'You know her?' the woman asked Mila.

'Of course,' Mila replied impatiently, 'she is Reb Zal – she was – is – wait, Judith, wait for me!'

Atara let go of Mila's arm. 'Go with her.'

Mila hesitated.

'Go,' Atara urged, 'don't leave her alone. Tell her I'll wait for her – go!'

Mila hurried into the synagogue.

In front of the angry woman still staring at her neckline, Atara hesitated. Perhaps it was not right to ask to greet Zalman if she was not dressed properly. Zalman would notice an immodest kerchief and a half-inch of exposed collarbone, and Atara must not be seen with Judith because then Atara's home in Manhattan would no longer be a sanctuary in which the girl could hide. Atara stepped back. She listened hard for the sound of Zalman's voice emerging from inside and then she zigzagged away between the strollers – not to cry, not before turning the corner, not to be seen sobbing, not in this street, not a sixty-four-year-old woman wearing an immodest kerchief and a collar a half-inch short of permitted.

★

JUDITH REACHED the front row of the women's balcony. She glued an eye to the lattice. Would seeing her betrothed make things clear?

Zalman Stern was shaking hands with Grandpa Josef — Zalman Stern come from Paris to officiate at his grandson's wedding, her wedding, and there were her brothers, there was her Yoel behind Grandpa Josef — *Please God, is Yoel Stern my b'shert? HaShem, guide me: Can Yoel Stern and Judith Halberstamm form a righteous couple in Israel? HaShem, if you remain silent, may I remain silent?*

Zalman stepped up onto the central dais.

Josef's hand slid to his heart and his face went pale.

Judith gripped the lattice. Was Grandpa Josef dying?

Zalman's voice rose, *'Splendid is His Honour . . .'*

Josef leaned back and rested his head on the pillows that propped him up in his wheelchair. His eyes closed.

Zalman's notes climbed higher and the men's chests swelled with longing. In the balcony, women started to sob. Zalman's still-climbing notes stirred Judith's yearning to be pure and white and near the Creator, near the warmth of the Lord's golden presence. Her pale, bluish eyelids closed like a book.

The singing stopped, her eyes opened.

Zalman Stern was stepping down from the dais. The men formed a circle around Zalman and Josef, a singing dancing circle. Zalman's hand came to rest on Josef's shoulder; Josef's hand came to rest on Zalman's hand; Yoel pushed Josef's wheelchair — so they circled for one round.

Zalman returned to the raised platform and stood facing the Lord, and the entire congregation turned and stood facing the Lord; the men below and the women in the gallery. Again Zalman's voice rose, to

chant the passage read in every synagogue on the
Festival of the Law, the passage that concludes the last
book of the Pentateuch:

*And Moses went up ... to the top of Pisgah, that is
over against Jericho, and the Lord showed him all
the land ... and the Lord said unto him ... thou shalt
not go over thither ... The Promised Land thou shalt
not enter.*

Judith heard the Lord's verdict.

'Yoel and Judith *you shall not enter,*' she whispered, and
coupling the two names also felt forbidden.

The men completed the final few verses, then they
raised the Torah scroll to turn it back to *In the Beginning.*

And it was wound within that scroll:

לא יבא ממזר בקהל ה׳

*A mamzer shall not enter the Congregation of
the Lord*

Judith unfastened the clasp of her pearl necklace,
Yoel's present, that she had already chosen as her sign to
let him know when she would be permitted. She placed
the necklace next to the prayer book and stepped away
from the lattice. The women pressing forward to see
Zalman Stern jostled her to the back of the gallery. Judith
wound her way down the stairs and into the street,
between the strollers and mothers. She turned the corner.

★

MILA SHOULDERED her way to the front row of the women's balcony. She looked left and right but did not see Judith. She stood up on a pew's bench. Other women, too, stood on benches, to catch a glimpse of the dance below. Mila scanned the sea of white kerchiefs searching for Judith's dark hair. She held on to the pew's back and steadied herself. Again she scanned the balcony. She climbed down the bench, precipitously, and was caught by two women. Her arms extended to push aside the crowd. She stood at the top of the staircase, but could not see the girl's head among the bobbing scarves. She pushed her way down the stairs and into the street.

The synagogue's side door opened. A throng in black coats came rushing out. 'Room, make room!' The crowd parted and there was her Josef, slumped in his wheelchair. The wheelchair swivelled. Josef's hands tapped the air as if he were trying to situate himself, and the blue vein on Josef's temple throbbed, and the skin of his cheeks stretched like parchment.

Mila rushed to his side. 'What happened?'

A youth answered, 'The heat, there's no air inside.'

Mila was not listening. She was leaning close to Josef, whispering into his ear, 'What happened when you saw Zalman Stern? Did you speak?'

Josef reached for her hand. 'Milenka, I'm glad it's you.'

'Did you speak?'

Josef placed a hand on his chest. His other hand tapped the collar of Mila's dress, to calm her.

'Your heart?' Mila said.

Josef nodded, he smiled, nodded, and his lids half parted on his grey-green, unseeing eyes as he mouthed the word *lev*, heart.

'Lev?' Mila whispered.

Josef smiled.

It was a reading Josef had taught Rachel at the Sabbath table, a reading he later taught Judith and her siblings, how the last letter of the Torah, ל (lamed), and the first letter, ב (beth), spelled the word לב (lev), *heart*. It was a reading Josef remembered from long ago: Every year, לב, lev, *heart*, linked the end to the beginning.

Mila understood that Josef had resolved to place his heart, silently, before the Law: Josef had not spoken to Zalman and would not speak of the matter again.

Josef – who long ago had abandoned this world and was now preparing to abandon the next – laughed, softly, as his fingers stroked her collar, then he raised his hand and the door opened on the men's prayer hall and the boys wheeled Josef back into the dance.

Mila watched him disappear behind the black coats and biber hats. The door to the men's hall banged shut.

Now Mila was even more anxious to find Judith, to tell her that Josef, whom Judith so admired, had decided never to speak of it again. Mila rose on her toes and searched for Judith among the strollers and mothers. She crossed the street, stood on the opposite pavement, rushed from one corner to the other.

The tips of the mothers' white scarves fluttered between their shoulders in the late-summer breeze. She rushed past Landau's grocery, past the narrow Judaica store. Again she rose on her toes. 'Judith! Judith! Judith!'

★

JUDITH'S FIRST PAIR of heeled shoes, bought for her first meeting with Yoel, rapped the pavement. Clik-clak-clik, a kaleh meidel does not run, a girl in age of marriage pays heed to her deportment — on the Festival of the Law, when every danced step is a prayer, can a mamzer's steps, too, adorn the Lord's crown? Clik-clak-clik Judith ran from her forbidden self, a self forever forbidden to Yoel, a self permitted only to the forbidden — a sodden newspaper licked her ankle, she shook her leg but the wet paper clung to her calf, and the elevated track rattled with an approaching train — trains were forbidden on the Festival of the Law but Judith's hands clasped the bars of an exit gate, they pushed, pulled, shook, a voice called from the booth, her hands shook the bars harder, pushed, pulled — the gate buzzed and opened. There was yelling, and a thunder above, but clik-clak-clik the new shoes rapped the stairs, and the wide grey ledge quaked under her heels — Judith turned towards the rumble, towards the two horns of light,

הנני

hineni, *here I am*

there between the light and the sleeper, a cradle of dust for thou art dust, and Judith swung her arms back as her torso bowed forward, her knees flexed, her heels left the ground then her toes, so Judith danced off the platform.

She landed on the balls of her feet, on the first rail. Her arms lifted, she regained her balance and leaned into the two gleaming lines.

There was a loud blast of the horn, she saw the

mountain smoking, saw the sound and lightning as the thunder of the Law smashed into—

THE TRAIN stopped mid-station. Two bystanders advanced, slowly, towards where the girl had stood, towards the black shoe on the edge of the platform.

★

JOSEF LEARNED of Judith's end before the seventh round.

His open eyes were two grey-green clouds. He grieved for the ram the Lord had chosen, his hand on his chest, he grieved until the beat of his heart fell silent.

★

As soon as three stars were visible in the sky, women from the Burial Society ritually cleansed Judith's remains. They washed the dust and the dirt and the bodily fluids; they shrouded the remains in white cotton.

Men from the Burial Society ritually cleansed Josef's body and dressed it in white cotton.

The women from the Burial Society came to tear Mila's garment, close to her heart.

In the house of double mourning, the uninterrupted flow of visitors conjectured about the inexplicable death of a seventeen-year-old: Outsiders had been seen in the neighbourhood, a woman had tried to follow Mila and Judith into the synagogue. Had someone abducted Judith? Was Judith trying to escape when she fell onto the track? Why else would a girl from Williamsburg find herself near a train on a Holy Day? *Baruch dayan emeth, Blessed be the Judge of Truth.*

And Josef . . . Josef who could not bear the news of his granddaughter's death — *Blessed be the Judge of Truth.*

★

JUDITH'S MOTHER, Rachel, went into labour when she heard that the Lord took back her firstborn and her father on one same day.

Rachel gave birth to her eleventh child, her sixth son.

Zalman ruled that it was permissible to wish mazel tov to these mourners, because the birth of a child is good news.

A little girl found Judith's pearls in the women's balcony, next to a prayer book.

Judith's mother hugged her newborn and swayed back and forth on her mourning stool. 'How could her necklace have fallen off?' bewildered Rachel murmured in her grief. 'My Yuditel was so fond of those pearls, a gift from her fiancé, my poor Judith who came into this world on such a lucky date, the twenty-first of the month of Kislev . . .'

On the mourning stool next to Rachel sat Mila. The pearls clicked in her trembling hands. 'The clasp must not have held,' Mila whispered even as she pictured Judith's fingers lifting the necklace to her lips, unfastening the hook, closing the prayer book with a last kiss.

THE COVENANT of Circumcision was incised on the newborn's flesh on his eighth day, and Rachel named her sixth son Josef, in memory of her father, Josef Lichtenstein, whose name was not erased from the generations.

★

THE PHONE rang in Atara's loft. 'Burn it, burn it to ashes,' Mila said. 'No, don't come, Rachel's children must be safe. No, you mustn't come . . . there is a rumour that a woman abducted Judith . . . some woman, a stranger, but if they recognised you – You will burn it?'

One day earlier, the girl had curled up on Atara's coverlet, her pale eyelids flickering . . .

Atara burned Mila's notebook in a large pot over the stove, she burned it to ashes.

★

A YEAR LATER, Mila called to say that Hannah was not well.

Atara took the first flight to Paris where she had not settled even after she was of age, in order to spare her parents the shame of an apostate daughter in their city.

Mila begged Zalman: Atara should be permitted to come into the house to see her ailing mother, but Zalman rose on his bad knees. 'YEMACH SHEMEAH!' he bellowed. *Let her name be erased* – once more he made himself curse the heretic child with nonexistence.

Her siblings arranged for Atara to come when Zalman would be out of the house.

Alone in her hotel room, waiting for the phone to ring, Atara thought of the blank writing pads on her one tidy shelf, pages ivory or china white; her unwritten letters to Hannah. She had even daydreamed she might write to Zalman, and more unwritten pages had joined the stack of unsent mail, unused stamps.

Some of the pages were not entirely white:

Chère Maman,

followed by the cursive acronym for *Until One Hundred and Twenty Years,*

Chère Maman, עמו"ש
How are you?
I am fine.

Below, the page was empty. If she were happy, how could she explain happiness far from her family? If she were unhappy, had they not warned her?

The window of her hotel room gave onto an ivy-covered wall full of twittering birds. One flew off, two others returned and disappeared in the dense leafage.

Atara thought of the day, one year earlier, when she had tried to find her way back to Manhattan after leaving Mila and Judith, after the angry woman had stopped her from entering the synagogue. Atara had searched for a taxi, for the wallet she had not taken with her, not to offend Judith — muktza, the wallet was muktza on the Festival of the Law — she had climbed the pedestrian

ramp to the Williamsburg Bridge. The trestle had struggled with an oncoming train, she had kept walking, half
slumped over the handrail, hoping the girl might still
come.

She leapt to the phone. Mila was on the line; Zalman
would be out all afternoon.

Atara rushed to Hannah's bedside.

Hannah beamed and took Atara's hand as if no time
had passed. Hannah could not speak easily because an
oxygen mask covered her nose and mouth, but she
pointed to her floral-print apron, draped over the back
of a chair. When Atara brought it to her, Hannah
pointed to the pockets. Atara retrieved scraps of ruled
paper torn from an old school notebook, scraps that
Hannah had filled with tight Yiddish cursive, unsent
messages that begged a daughter to return to her *Jewish
home,* begged a daughter to remember a mother who
longed to press her child to her bosom. Atara wiped her
nose and eyes. Hannah clasped her daughter's hand and
hummed, *A letter to your mother . . . send it express . . . a
brief letter to your mother, my child . . . a fine Hasid we
have for you . . .*

Hannah's eyes still waited for Atara to come back, her
ears still waited to hear, before the end, Atara ask the
Lord for forgiveness and pledge to obey His Law.

So the river wept on the windowpane, wept the impossible return.

Etti rushed in; Zalman was on his way.

Atara kissed Hannah's cheeks and hand, she left
Hannah's bedside and tried not to wish Zalman dead. She
reached the Luxembourg Gardens. She went to the playground of her summers with Mila. Stone folds cupped
the marble breasts of the queens of France who stood

guard around the pond she had circled with Mila on the bicycle.

The Sénat bell rang the quarter hour.

Should she have fought for Mila? Should she have insisted that Mila accompany her to the library? But if Mila, too, had left, who would have consoled Hannah and Zalman?

Should she have fought for Judith against Judith's will?

The sound of a rake combing the gravel soothed Atara's disarray. Silence trailed the rake. Autumn leaves settled in the wheelbarrow.

Transylvania

IT WAS A PILGRIMAGE ATARA HAD LONG MEANT TO make, to see how it was, back there, without Jews. She needed to feel the absence.

She told Mila about the planned trip and Mila sent the brooch that had belonged to Josef's mother.

Atara called Mila. 'How will I find her?'

Mila described a horse meadow along a railway track that followed a river, a linden tree by a wooden gate, a chicken coop, a cowshed.

'But you never heard from her?' Atara asked.

'We sent parcels. For years, I ran down to the mailbox, hoping for a letter from Florina, hoping to greet Josef, may he rest in peace, with the good news. No letter arrived. We sent parcels until a recent émigré from Romania told Josef that it might not be a good idea; in Ceauşescu's Romania, Florina might be interrogated about her contacts with the West. Josef was beside himself with worry. I tried to reassure him, corrupt customs officers confiscated the parcels, she never even knew we sent them, thugs stole the sugar and the coffee – we never heard from her.'

After wishing Atara well on her journey, Mila added: 'I accompanied your father on a pilgrimage to the Rebbe's tomb, in upstate New York. I saw him include your name, *Eydell Atara,* on the note he inserted in the tombstone. He wrote your name on the top of the page, because you were his firstborn, then he wrote out the names of your siblings. He included you among his children, for whom he prayed that the Lord show kindness and mercy.'

★

THE WIND rushed past as Atara stood near the open window in the narrow corridor. The eastbound train rumbled through places that had once been home; Vienna, Prague, Budapest, Warsaw . . . She had imagined blue-black digits scarring the land indelibly; it seemed only she was scarred.

Along tracks that smelled of dust, metal and urine, she hummed Hannah's songs; on the worn benches of Europe's market squares, she hummed old melodies to hush broken hearts and move them on, *Es brent, briderlech es brent . . .* She hummed softly for souls that still haunt those river-banks, disoriented souls that cannot find trace of their existence. The tunes floated in squares emptied of Jews as she boarded yet another train to more erased traces.

She reached Transylvania and disembarked at the Satu Mare station. Small letters below the sign for Satu Mare indicated that the locality had also been known as Szatmár. She took a taxi to the main square of Satu Mare / Szatmár, to the Piaţa Libertăţii. Leaning against sooty pillars, heavily made-up women in tiny skirts crossed and uncrossed their bare legs, high heels tap-tapping the cold stone. She asked whether a synagogue still stood in Satu Mare.

Yes, but there was no congregation.

She made her way to the border that had separated northern Transylvania from southern Transylvania during the war, she thought of Mila and her parents locked inside a synagogue, packing the same suitcase thirty-one days; she thought of the night the Jews of Deseu took leave of their river, how the farmers among them worried about the seeds that had not been planted, and the mothers told of daisy-dappled fields, and the children fell asleep while the river scored their breath, one last night.

She found Deseu and its Jewish cemetery. She looked for the grave of Mila's father but the stones leaned side-ways and some had fallen entirely and she could not tell whose grave was whose.

She heard Judith's lament; she heard Josef's lullaby consoling the lament:

Will I corrupt the seed of Zalman Stern?
Hie lee lu lee la ...

An old man stepped out of a birch grove. 'Are you a Jewish? Evreu?'

The man decided this woman must be, standing there among the graves. He smiled an impish smile and in his threadbare, Soviet-era coat, with his mouth emptied of teeth, he sang, *'Yadidadidam!'*

He unfolded a greyish napkin on a stone and placed upon it a few plastic barrettes, a bookmark with a photograph of a synagogue, safety pins, portraits of saints . . . 'Cheap, very cheap!'

Atara gave him some money and left the cemetery.

She found the linden tree by the gate, the yard with the cowshed, the chicken coop.

An ancient, stooped woman in black kerchief and black dress shuffled towards her, a watering can in her hands. 'Hello, who are you?' the woman asked.

'I . . . I came— Josef . . . Josef Lichtenstein . . .'

'Shh . . .' The old woman placed a finger on her lips.

In the shadow of the linden tree where Zalman had stood half a century before, Atara started again: 'Anghel, I came to speak of Anghel.'

The woman's gnarled hand went to her pocket. She retrieved a wrinkled postcard and held it out.

Anghel had written to Florina that he would send for her when he had ploughed the fields of America.

The woman wiped an eye, slid the cracked postcard between the folds of her black skirt, looked up. 'Hello, who are you?'

Atara spoke of Anghel's marriage to the beautiful Mila Heller whose parents had lived near Cluj, across the river. She spoke of Anghel's love for his two mothers.

The woman raised the watering can. The water flowed from the spout, some inside the potted nettle.

Atara opened her purse and took out the brooch. 'Anghel would have wanted Florina to have this.'

The old woman eyed the brooch uncertainly.

Atara asked whether Florina had married, after Anghel had left.

The woman raised her clouded eyes. 'Hello, who are you?'

Atara entered the yard and pinned the brooch on the woman's lapel. The woman hummed to herself. When she noticed Atara again, she said, 'Hello?'

Atara started down the dirt road. Quacking ducks waddled after her as she pressed on, past doorways where mothers stood with tightened shawls around their shoulders and called through the lanes for children to come home.

Williamsburg, Brooklyn

MILA WAKES IN HER CHAIR BY THE LIVING-ROOM window. She leans forward and looks out. Among the sidecurls and the black coat flaps waving on the overpass, she searches for the messiah's white donkey, the sign that Josef and Judith live again. She hushes her great-grandchildren running circles around her armchair and listens for Elijah's step. She buries her face in her prayer book. *If my time comes before the messiah, may I be worthy of sojourning near my Josef, in the house of the pious* . . . She dozes off as her great-grandchildren laugh and spin their flyaway silken hair around her. One last time, Mila dreams of Josef placing a hand over his heart, a hand over her heart, and mouthing the word.

Glossary

ammah: phallus

apikores (pl. apikorsim): nonbeliever

apikorsus: heresy

baraita: Jewish oral law not incorporated into the six orders of the Mishnah

baruch habah (fem.): Beruchach habooah, literally: blessed be he (she) who comes – meaning: welcome

ben Torah: literally, son of Torah, a boy who behaves according to Torah precepts

biber hat: beaver hat; a 'flat', wide-brimmed black felt hat worn by Satmar men

challilah: God forbid

Debout les damnés de la terre: Arise you wretched of the earth

Eibershter: the one above, God

El maleh rachamim: God full of compassion; prayer for the dead, for the soul of the departed

haphtorah: excerpts from Prophets; traditionally read as part of the bar mitzvah ceremony

HaShem: literally: The Name; God

ilui: Torah prodigy

kaleh meidel: girl in age of marriage

lilin: demons

mitzvah: commandment; refers to the 613 commandments in the Torah; has also come to refer to an act of kindness

muktza: set aside; objects that may not be touched or moved on the Sabbath

phylactery: see under *tefilin*

Rebbe: leader of a Hasidic sect

sheigets: a young man, pejorative; a lowlife; also, a non-Jewish youth

shemah: considered the most important prayer in Judaism: *Hear, O Israel: the Lord is our God, the Lord is One*

shtreimel: fur hat of seven or thirteen sable tails, worn by married Hasidic men

shul: house of prayer

Simchath Torah: festival that celebrates the Torah

tefilin, phylacteries: a set of small leather boxes containing Hebrew text on vellum, worn by men at morning prayer, and the leather straps for tying them

T'nach: Book of Scripture

treifenah medinah: unkosher country

Acknowledgements

Scott Moyers and Andrew Wylie of the Wylie Agency responded to my over-the-transom manuscript and have my trust and admiration.

Lindsay Sagnette and Becky Hardie are extraordinary editors and supporters. I am grateful for the new literary community they are building at Hogarth, together with Maya Mavjee, Molly Stern, Clara Farmer, David Drake, Rachel Rokicki, Rachelle Mandik, Barbara Sturman, Christine Kopprasch, Rachel Meier, Julie Cepler and Jay Sones.

Florence Berger, Toby Berger, Julie Hilden, Heather White and David Coleman are the sort of readers every writer hopes for.

At different stages in the creation of this work, Adam Eaglin, John Casey, Maribelle Leavitt, Stephen Leavitt, Melanie Thernstrom, Sherry King and Deborah Reck gave me important feedback and encouragement.

Larry Berger read every draft from the first short story in English to the galleys.

HOGARTH

LONDON · NEW YORK

In 1917 Virginia and Leonard Woolf started The Hogarth Press from their Richmond home, Hogarth House, armed only with a hand-press and a determination to publish the newest, most inspiring writing. They went on to publish some of the twentieth century's most significant writers, joining forces with Chatto & Windus in 1946.

Inspired by their example, Hogarth is a new home for a new generation of literary talent; an adventurous fiction imprint with an accent on the pleasures of storytelling and a broad awareness of the world. Hogarth is a partnership between Chatto & Windus in the UK and the Crown Publishing Group in the US, and comes at a time when innovations in publishing and digital media are shrinking the world we share. Hogarth novels will be published as transatlantic events from London and New York.